Total-E-Bound Publishing books by Genella DeGrey:

Love Divine
Masterpiece
Whisked Away
Sins of the Flesh

I0569919

A TOUCH OF DESTINY

GENELLA DeGREY

A Touch of Destiny
ISBN # 978-1-78184-552-7
©Copyright Genella deGrey 2012
Cover Art by Posh Gosh ©Copyright June 2012
Interior text design by Claire Siemaszkiewicz
Total-E-Bound Publishing

Published in 2012 by Total-E-Bound Publishing, Think Tank, Ruston Way, Lincoln, LN6 7FL, United Kingdom.

A TOUCH OF DESTINY

Dedication

I would like to dedicate A Touch of Destiny, to the town of Tombstone, AZ and the ghosts that even today haunt the saloons, hotels and streets of The Town Too Tough To Die.

Chapter One

Late spring, Tombstone, Arizona Territory, 1880

"Where is she?" Beatrice demanded in a resolute voice as her gaze slid from the dirty, pink carpet bag on the floor next to the bed to the face of her husband of eight years. She recognised the anger in his eyes and nearly recoiled. He never appreciated it when she pointed out his faults – in fact, it was times such as these when he chose to teach his disrespectful wife a harsh lesson with the back of his hand, as his self-justified Christian duty dictated – but never in view of another living soul. Regardless of the consequences, Beatrice would stand her ground this time. The ugly little carpet bag may as well come to life and announce to the world that her spouse had brought a whore into their home.

She watched as his fists clenched and unclenched at his sides. Almost imperceptibly, his eyes darted to the armoire then back to her face.

"You are supposed to be at church." Failing to sound casual he added in a panic, "I've done nothing wrong!"

"Truly?" she turned to the pine wardrobe and shouted at the closed doors, "If everyone in this room is so innocent, then why the need to hide?" A flash of hope that she was

7

indeed mistaken shot through her mind. If a scandal such as this escaped the walls of their humble cottage, it would topple the very foundation of the church where her husband, Pastor Lindley Gaitland, preached.

"Cease, Beatrice," he warned, his tone hinting at the violence that lined his skin like an expensive, well-tailored suit. "Go and wait in the parlour."

Lindley's dismissal of her only proved his guilt. Beatrice's belly trembled with her indignation. She turned back to her husband. "How dare you defile our bed with some strumpet." she whispered unevenly, unable to draw enough air into her lungs to speak with the fury she felt.

"I said, into the parlour," he growled and drew back his hand.

She blinked, fully expecting to feel his fist across her face. Of course, were she to confront him with his actions at a later time, he would most likely make up some feeble excuse such as he'd only meant to assist her to the next room. Hindsight had told her years ago that she'd made her bed when she'd married a self-righteous, judgemental, delusional snake in the grass. And to the list she could now add 'cheating'.

At that very moment, their attention transferred to the doors to the armoire as they flew open and a naked, hefty, blonde woman spilled onto the floor.

Beatrice's modest sensibilities, which were not only ingrained into her by her East Coast society upbringing, but also demanded by her position as a minister's wife, caused her to turn away. She glanced up at Lindley who looked as if he were in pain. She imagined he must be, having his sin exposed in such a way.

Like a blow to her stomach, a realisation hit her. His humiliation infected her as if it were a germ they exchanged between one another. Angry, hurt and defeated, she escaped the oppressive room, retiring to the parlour as her husband had commanded.

Not long after Beatrice had shakily lowered herself to their shabby settee, the blonde woman, holding the sparse, dingy trappings of a typical mining camp whore against her body, ran from the bedroom to flee the cottage via the front door.

Anticipating her husband's wrath, she waited a full hour before venturing into the bedroom to receive her punishment. When she did, she found Lindley sprawled, belly up, on the floor at the foot of the bed, his face displaying a deathly pallor.

She ran to fetch Doctor Matthews.

Beatrice gasped as she sat up in bed, having been plucked from a recurring dream. The flash of lightning through the window lent the room a blue glow, but then faded to black just as quickly. The wrath-filled thunder rolled over her roof. Her late husband had been dead six months to the day, but her nightmares of that fateful evening had not let her be since the funeral. She'd often thought it might have been Lindley coming back to haunt her.

Hanging her feet over the side of the bed, she placed her toes on the cool, wooden floor and tiptoed over to the window. Another flash illuminated her face's reflection in the glass. "So much lightning, never the perfect amount of rain," she murmured to an empty room.

She pressed her forehead against the windowsill and thought of the poor miners having to endure the electrical storm from inside their flimsy tents. She shivered.

Turning from the window, she climbed back into bed. She could have used a warm body to curl up with on nights like this. A dog would have done just fine, but she couldn't afford a pet. And, besides, the breeds she'd grown up with at home in Rhode Island were not available out here, in the untamed West.

A growling stomach reminded her she'd eaten only one meal earlier that day. It had been given to her by one of Lindley's church members. Regular congregational offerings had stopped several weeks ago. She couldn't expect them to take care of her forever. In the interim, she'd been awaiting a second letter from the bank, informing her of when the small amount of money she'd originally been allowed would become unfrozen. If her late husband hadn't left every last thing they'd owned to his younger brother, she wouldn't be in this predicament.

Perhaps tomorrow she would go into town and ask for credit at the general store. Although she had refrained from doing so before, this last resort had now become essential. She knew without a doubt that Mr McElroy, the owner, would appreciate her plight and lend his assistance.

Her plans to fall back asleep until dawn were fraught with folly. It was likely she'd toss and turn fitfully for the remainder of the night.

* * * *

The sun rose on Sunday, its light seeming brighter than usual as it slowly invaded Beatrice's room. She made her bed and focused on the task of dressing in her good mourning gown, hoping to find a bite to eat in town.

Suddenly, the bell at the Shepherd of the Hills Church, where her late husband used to preach, rang. Loud and clear.

"Who in the world?" Beatrice tied her widow's bonnet under her chin, tossed her black shawl over her shoulders, and hurried along the mile or so to the tent that served as the Shepherd of the Hills Church. It promised to be another hot day, but curiosity overruled her ponderings over the weather.

She entered and found that her late husband's younger brother, Allen Gaitland, had aired out the tent and dusted off the benches. "Allen?"

"Ah, there is my darling sister-in-law!" He reached out and tugged her into an embrace. "Did you get my flowers at the funeral?"

She pulled out of his arms. "Yes, thank you. What are you doing here?"

Allen smiled down at her. "All of your questions will be answered at the meeting. How many usually attend?"

"Er, around twenty or so. But this little mining camp is booming and people pour into town all week long. Are you —?" Her mind raced, but she was unable to find civil words to verbalise her feelings. *What is he talking about? What meeting?*

"Praise God. All the more souls to save." He smirked, his glistening green eyes so very similar to his brother's.

She had no idea how to react to his declaration. Last she'd heard, Allen sold hair brushes door to door. He certainly wasn't a pastor. Forcing her lips into a pleasant smile, she nodded. "Praise God." She turned away, but made an entire circle in order to find her voice and face him again. "Allen, why would you hold a meeting? You aren't a pastor."

"Don't you worry about a thing, Beatrice. If my brother could do it, it shouldn't be that difficult."

Beatrice pivoted on her heel and paced past a few rows of benches before she closed her gaping jaw. Once again, he'd left her speechless.

* * * *

After Allen's 'sermon', Beatrice waited and watched as 'Pastor Allen'—that was what he had asked everyone to call him—bade farewell to the church attendants. The way that people took to him and his brother were eerily similar.

Allen stood a half-foot shorter than her late husband, his hair finer and fairer. They had nearly the same beguiling smile, which made people want to be around them, want to follow them anywhere. *Charisma* was the word that best described what the brothers had. As she observed the mood of the congregation, the men looked as if they wanted Allen as their closest friend, and the women slid envious glances her way. Both Lindley and Allen were charmingly handsome in their own manner, but, recalling Lindley's angry side, she shuddered.

Allen gained her attention, snapping her out of her thoughts. "May I escort you back home, my dear?"

"Certainly," she smiled and took his proffered elbow, wishing she could gather the courage to approach the subject of his new career. Instead, she conversed with her brother-in-law about everything from his journey to the weather in Tombstone. When they topped the last of the low, rolling hills on the way to her cottage, she confessed to the limited hospitality of her kitchen at present. "I would invite you in for lunch. However, my funds have been frozen by the bank. I can't get anyone to tell me why."

Allen smiled at her. "Then perhaps I can provide a miracle for you."

Beatrice turned and looked into his eyes, hoping with all her heart that what he suggested could be accomplished.

"The assets will be unfrozen by the time we get into town."

"How?" Taken aback, she nearly misstepped on the dirt path before her.

Steadying her, Allen replied, "I have written to the bank, informing them of my arrival. As you know, I am the executor of Lindley's will."

Of course, she thought to herself flatly. This was something she hadn't forgotten — not since the reading of the will. She nodded for him to go on.

"I shall arrange for an allowance to be paid to you, weekly if you find it sufficient."

She relaxed her shoulders. "Oh, Allen, you've saved my life," she exclaimed with vigour, smiling up at him.

He patted her fingers, which were entrapped in the crook of his arm. "We'll get groceries for you, then you can cook me a meal. How does that sound?"

Relieved she would have food in the house once again, she agreed. "Will you be staying at the cottage, then?"

Allen's face displayed a look of admiration. "No, no. I don't wish to intrude." Before she could protest, he finished. "I'll be happily ensconced at the Grand Hotel until other arrangements can be made."

Grateful to the depths of her soul, she said, "Thank you so much, Allen. Your generosity means the world to me."

* * * *

Later in the afternoon, when the dishes from Allen's meal were cleaned and put away, Beatrice set herself to the task of preparing for Stone Soup Hour. The Stone Soup Hour was a church-based, community-supported meal that served the people of meagre means around camp. Every Sunday evening at the Shepherd of the Hills tent, she fed the hungry. She would gather offerings from businesses about town — poultry, rabbit — any kind of stewing meat. She'd gladly accept cabbage, potatoes and any vegetables they were willing to spare, extra broth from the Grand Hotel's pantry, and spices from the general store.

She borrowed a wheelbarrow from Mr McElroy, owner-operator of the general store, wrestled the large cauldron and tri-post hanger from her own kitchen onto it, and went from door to door, obtaining soup donations.

The struggling miners and less fortunate in the area would be pleased with tonight's stone soup. The fare would be a wonderful, hearty chicken broth and vegetable stew. Not only did she get a large helping of chicken stock from the hotel and a crate full of healthy, unblemished root vegetables, but she had also gathered a few leaves of fresh basil and a long sprig of rosemary from her own paltry herb garden.

Beatrice smiled. No one would call it slop tonight. Then again, the only one who ever had was her late husband Lindley, and never in public. She sobered as she approached the meeting tent. He'd fooled them all, hiding his true self, and keeping the secret of his dark soul for his wife alone. In Lindley's eyes, he'd followed the Good Book to the letter, believing it was everyone else who was doomed to burn in hell.

Knowing it to be indecorous to speak ill of the dead, she shrugged off her negative thoughts, but kept in mind that the truth could be cruel from time to time.

* * * *

The sparks from her flint stone took to the dried brush and wood pile in an instant. It wasn't long before the cauldron was bubbling as it dangled above the blaze, and she began chopping vegetables, sliding them from her little cutting board into the broth-steeped herbs.

One of the girls from the congregation, Virginia Clark, approached the makeshift kitchen.

"Hello, Ginny," Beatrice hailed her young friend and smiled. "I'm so glad you came out to assist me again."

"So," Ginny said, rubbing her hands in anticipation, "what can I do, Mrs Gaitland?"

"What else?"

"Stir the pot!" both of them chimed simultaneously then giggled.

Ginny took up the large, wooden spoon and Beatrice made small talk with her. She would have taken an oath that her freckle-faced, chestnut-haired, fourteen-year-old friend had grown about a half-foot, and was on the verge of developing a fine woman's figure since she'd come to know her. It was a pity indeed that the young lady's education was limited to a one-room, all-age-encompassing schoolhouse in Tombstone.

"I'm so pleased your mother allows you to help me out. Honestly," Beatrice lowered her voice to a more intimate level, "I can't help but suspect you oblige me because of the loss of Pastor Gaitland," she commented, half kidding. She'd been curious before, but had never broached the subject. Now that they had known each other as friends for some weeks, she thought it a good time to ask.

"Naw. Ma has always needled me to come and volunteer, but I didn't much like the looks of the old —" Ginny stopped herself from speaking further. "I'm sorry, Mrs Gaitland. I didn't mean —"

Beatrice smiled to quell her young friend's discomfort. "There is no need, Ginny. It's all right." *I understand completely.* Thankfully, Beatrice caught herself before she vocalised her thoughts. She dropped her gaze to concentrate on the vegetables. Children and animals were very perceptive when it came to her late husband. They'd shied away from him far more often than adults had done.

They both looked up as a man, holding a bowl with a pair of dead chickens, the heads and feet sticking up, spilling over the top, walked towards them, his face bowed as if he were focusing on the path before him.

"He's here again," Ginny murmured.

"Who?"

"The one who smoulders when he looks at you. He was here last week—"

"Ginny Clark. You shouldn't say—oh, now hush or he'll hear us." Beatrice cleared her throat. "Can I help you?" she asked him in a friendly manner, and slid more vegetables into the pot.

As if in slow motion, he raised his head. From under his hat, his striking, crystalline blue eyes greeted hers, his bashful smile prompting a dimple to cut into his left cheek.

The vision before her almost caused Beatrice to lose the grip she had on the knife. Her mouth went dry. Her lungs ceased to function.

Apparently, a trace of the divine had decided to walk among mortals this evening.

Chapter Two

Touching the brim of his hat in what the West thought of as a proper greeting, he spoke to Beatrice.

"Hello, ma'am, miss." He sent a polite glance Ginny's way. "These chickens are from Bauer's meat market, for the supper tonight."

Taking a breath, she nodded. "Thank you, mister—"

"You can call me Luke."

Perceiving his youth in comparison to her own age, Beatrice didn't feel uncomfortable using his given name, even though he couldn't have been too much younger than she. Moreover, she refused to include his striking good looks into the equation. "Luke. Thank you." She turned to Ginny. "Take the chickens and—"

"Uh," he interrupted, "I wouldn't mind dressing the varmints for you."

Beatrice grinned at the funny way he'd spoken of the meat. "All right, Luke, pluck away."

He pinched the brim of his hat again and made his way towards where the stream ran, snake-like, at the bottom of the hill.

"Cousins and corsets, I ain't never seen a finer lookin' man." Ginny beamed the moment Luke stepped out of hearing range.

Beatrice turned to her young companion. "If your mother were to hear you talk in such a manner—"

"She'd agree in a heartbeat! Did you see those straight, white teeth and that silky blond hair? Did I mention his wide shoulders?"

"He had an agreeable smile," she offered as she sliced into a potato, staring unseeing at it, and keeping her face as still as a statue's. Ginny's accurate observations nearly caused girlish giggles to bubble up from her very depths, and if Beatrice gave in she'd be obliged to confess her own reflections when asked—and there wasn't the slightest doubt that Ginny *would* ask.

"His smile wasn't the only thing agreeable, Mrs Gaitland. You watched him walk away, same as I did."

This time, a squawk of laughter almost escaped her. "That will be enough, dear. Ladies don't say things like that aloud. It would behove you to remember such," she said in a maternal tone, although the grand cathedral bells were not quite finished ringing in her head from the encounter.

"Yer right. I should'a just mentioned his beautiful mouth and be done with it."

"Ginny!"

"What? It was. Why, kissin' him would be—"

Beatrice actually choked before she found her voice. "Good heavens, Ginny! Where did you learn of such things?"

"Well, I was over behind the Bird Cage one day, and—"

To be honest, Beatrice didn't want to hear her answer. "Just never mind."

"Now, Mrs Gaitland, a gal could come by some valuable particulars listenin' to the whores talk about—"

"That will be all on the subject, dear."

"But yer always sayin' how important an education is and those women *really* know a thing or two—"

"A lady doesn't speak about... Oh, go on into the tent now, and set the benches."

Although slightly perturbed—the emotion revealed by the sour look on her face—Ginny did as she was told.

Beatrice lowered her gaze to the ground. "Children these days." She shook her head.

Had he really attended last week, and she hadn't noticed him then? The thought seemed impossible to her. But, for heaven's sake—she shook herself mentally—Stone Soup Hour was not meant to be a place to stir up a courtship.

Pushing her meandering thoughts aside, she stood and added the newly cubed vegetables to the cauldron.

Not long after, Luke came back and handed her the bowl of meat.

"I wondered where you'd got off to." She peered into the bowl and found she barely recognised its contents. "What have you done to the chicken?" She looked up at him for his answer.

Luke shrugged. "I went ahead and took out the bones and other undesirables."

"Oh," she said, and glanced into the bowl once again. "How kind of you." Unable to remain under his intense gaze, she occupied herself with spooning the meat and skin into the pot.

From the corner of her eye, she watched him inspect the area around the tent.

When his attention returned to her, he took a step closer to the fire and asked quietly, "Have we met before?"

Beatrice couldn't bring herself to face him, owing to what she deemed to be a rather forward question coming from a stranger, not to mention the way his voice had rolled down her arms, she answered, "No, sir. I have not seen you around these parts, and I've been living here for some time now." Standing, she excused herself, set the bowl on a nearby bench and strode into the tent.

Wringing her hands against the irrational trembling, she called to Ginny who was at present arranging the seats for the guests. At Stone Soup Hour, they liked to sit in circles as opposed to rows as if they were in church.

Ginny looked up from across the tent. "Over here, Mrs Gaitland."

"Ginny, I need you to come out and stir the stew." She'd sort of lied, but she could not go back out there alone with that beautiful man hovering over her like a bee buzzing around nectar. "Go on, I will finish up in here."

Ginny nodded knowingly. "He's back, then."

"Who?"

"You know who, *Luke*."

The young girl's voice dipped towards the seductive, but Beatrice ignored it. "Yes, the meat is cooking now."

Ginny walked over to where Beatrice stood. "Last Sunday, it seemed he always had his eye on you – at every moment he knew where you were, what you were doin'. I tried to point it out to you then, but you'd been so occupied with the stew…"

"Nonsense, Ginny. You have an overactive imagination, that's all. Now go on and give the cauldron a stir or two."

Ginny harrumphed, a very grown-up sound to Beatrice's ears. As Ginny took her leave, she felt the girl's gaze upon her back, but didn't turn to acknowledge it.

* * * *

While sunset coloured the sky with bright oranges, reds and twilight blues, the clearing next to the Shepherd of the Hills Church tent filled with hungry miners, each with his own tin cup or bowl. It was these poor miners — the ones that hadn't found their fortune yet — who plucked at Beatrice's heart strings. These men weren't the kind to loaf about, expecting to be taken care of — they were hard-working, toiling daily to carve out a living.

She'd never considered herself an overly religious person, not even after she'd married Lindley. Of course she believed in God, but her convictions dictated to her a more personal ministry. She wanted to do her little part to help her fellow man, even if it was feeding them once a week.

"Smells good, Mrs Gaitland."

"Can hardly wait, ma'am."

A few of the congregated delicately encouraged her to declare supper ready.

She checked once more to make sure the meat was fully cooked, then looked to the gathering. "All right, gentlemen, chow's on," she said with a friendly smile.

Doling out the aromatic stew, she accepted their thanks with quiet grace.

The miners filed into the tent, where lanterns had been lit for the evening meal. As the final man in line approached the cauldron, Beatrice looked up to see Luke standing just beyond him. It almost seemed as if Luke had lingered in anticipation of being the last man in the queue. But that was impossible. Wasn't it?

"There was no need for you to wait, Luke. You did participate in the preparations, you know."

He shrugged a shoulder and held out his bowl, smiling. "I'm not in any hurry. Besides, I like to watch you." He'd added the latter in a soft murmur.

Unused to straightforward interaction with the opposite sex, she pretended not to hear the second half of his comment. "Well, next time you get to be the first. I insist." The smile, which spread across her face, felt wooden as she spooned his meal into the proffered bowl.

Later, after seconds had been passed out, and the miners had departed, Ginny set the inside of the tent to rights. When she'd finished up, Beatrice shooed her on home. "See you next week, Ginny?"

Ginny waved in acknowledgement and departed down the path.

"How did your Stone Soup Hour turn out tonight? You had a hearty attendance, I trust?" Allen asked as he approached the fire from beyond its light.

Beatrice smiled. "We had a nice-sized crowd. Care for some? It's chicken and vegetables this time around."

"No, I'll wait until you cook me my very own supper tonight."

Not wishing to be rude, but hoping to discourage him from waiting for her to cook another meal, she looked him squarely in the eyes. "Allen," she began softly, "my Sunday night supper usually consists of what's left over from the pot." She indicated the cauldron.

Allen's eyebrows rose as if he was on the verge of pointing out her insolence, but, at the last possible moment, he relaxed. "I see. Well, I'll just go on over to the hotel then." He turned on his heel and disappeared, seeping back into the darkness past the light of the campfire.

She watched him go. And refused to feel guilty about not catering to his every need, even though he provided her with an allowance, but, for heaven's sake, she wasn't his wife.

"The man doesn't know what he's missing," a warm voice murmured.

She looked up to see Luke, exactly who she'd thought had spoken. He stood not five feet away as he watched her. Beatrice was flattered to the tips of her toes and her cheeks heated. He was awfully fine-looking, and thus far, hadn't ordered her around like the other men in her life.

"Thank you, Luke," she murmured humbly. It wasn't often she received praise of that calibre regarding her cooking. Then again, the compliment may have been dictated by his good manners. Waving away the stray thought, she indicated the pot. "There's more left over than I can eat. Would you care for seconds? I'd hate to see it go to waste."

"I'd love another helping, Mrs Gaitland. Your cooking is the best I've had out this way."

She smiled cordially and ladled another helping into his bowl. "So you aren't from around here?" she asked and slid to one end of a bench.

Luke claimed the empty bench space but hesitated with his answer. "Not—originally."

When he didn't continue, she dismissed his non-reaction, unwilling to pursue the subject if he was disinclined.

They huddled close to the dying fire. She spooned the last bits of stew into her mouth from the pot while Luke ate from his bowl.

Beatrice glanced at him from the corner of her eye and found him watching her with a look of intrigue. She shrugged. "I know it's not very ladylike of me, but I don't usually bring my eating implements."

A full smile blossomed across his face at her comment. He set down his bowl, and began to chuckle.

She paused with a spoonful of broth halfway to her mouth. "What?"

Luke reached into his waistcoat pocket and produced a handkerchief. He crooked his finger at her as he snapped open the folded, pristine cotton square. "It's not the eating implements which make up your plight."

She put her spoon down and looked at him, not quite sure what he wanted of her. Then he reached out and wiped the corner of her mouth.

"It's your deplorable manners," he murmured drily.

Uninhibited laughter burst forth from her. "Good heavens, Luke. I thought you were being serious."

He grinned. "Oh, I'm rarely that." He took her chin in his other hand to steady her face and his smile faded away. "You'll know for sure when I am."

At once his look became intense, as if to show her the difference. Returning his stare as he held her thus, she felt the napkin fall away, but his hand remained.

His gaze dropped to her mouth.

Her heart began to pound.

A soft pressure on her lower lip as his finger traced a line across it caused her entire body to heat, suggesting that, at any moment, she could burst into flames.

"Is it gone?" Exactly how she'd managed to form the query escaped her.

"Is what gone?" he asked above a whisper, as if he'd suddenly entered the conversation.

She swallowed. "The mess you dabbed from my face."

A nearly undetectable nod served as his answer.

"Then perhaps you should release me." Even to her own ears, her suggestion bore an audible resemblance to a question.

Luke's expression shifted from scorching to composed. "Of course."

At some point during their private exchange her appetite had fled. "I need to clean this up." She made to stand, but Luke rose before she could.

"Allow me," he offered. He took the cauldron handle in one hand and his bowl in the other, and headed towards the creek.

She could only stare after him, not knowing what to think of the situation. Lord, she'd known him for no more than three hours and would be happy to have his company on a cold night.

Where in the world had that thought come from? She stood abruptly and took a step to the right, then reversed directions and took two to the left.

Most likely from the fact that he nearly kissed you just now, a voice in the back of her mind answered.

In all her adult life she'd never been one to swoon or faint over a handsome face, and she wasn't about to let him bewilder her in such a way now. Squaring her shoulders, she marched into the tent, realigned the benches, doused the lamps, and tied the flaps down, chastising herself along the way. By the time she finished, Luke had returned with a clean cauldron.

"Thank you for the assistance tonight, Luke," she offered while dusting off her hands.

He set the tripod and cauldron into the wheelbarrow. "Glad to be of service, ma'am. However, I have one more thing to do."

Her heart quickened its pace. "And that is?"

He looked down at his boots for a moment then back up to her face from underneath the brim of his hat. "Walk you home."

He was utterly adorable when he acted shyly. There must be a dozen sides to this young man.

"Your accompaniment would suit me just fine, Luke," she said, unable to hold back her smile.

* * * *

"Lucas Hughson," he reprimanded himself from atop his bedroll at the base of the Dragoon Mountains. He shook his head. "You idiot." They'd never met before, and it didn't matter whether or not she looked a bit familiar to him.

"You utter fool."

Not only that, but she was the widow of a minister, for God's sake. "No offence," he murmured in the direction of the starlit sky.

He rested his head back upon his coat. "But, damn, is she *tempting*." He rolled over on to his side and looked, unseeing, into the brush beyond, a grin splitting his lips.

He'd come dangerously close to kissing her tonight. From the first time he'd seen her one week ago he'd wanted to do so. Since then, he was willing to gamble a stack of twenty-five dollar chips that, underneath her plain widow's weeds and bonnet, a body of pure feminine perfection lay in wait. The curve of her hips through her skirts was enough to drive him to drink. It promised a soft ride for the hard piece he toted between his legs — the one that was even now trying to painfully fight its way out of his pants at the mere thought of her naked thighs.

"Shit," he mumbled and unbuttoned his fly.

* * * *

Sitting up in bed, Beatrice found herself panting, having just awoken from a dream, a dream she'd had of Luke. She swiped the sleeve of her nightdress across her damp forehead, remembering the nature of the dream. He'd been kissing her and somehow, some way, she'd had one of those episodes between her legs, something she'd only attempted once in a while with her own hand, and much to her shame.

Beatrice looked down at her lap. Her legs were pressed together, ensconced in her nightdress, and tangled within her sheets. Not an inch of skin showed, therefore it was improbable that her hand could have strayed to the location where her desires, under normal circumstances, lay dormant.

The possibility was slim to none. Had it really happened?

She giggled. And so what if it had? It wasn't her doing if she'd been dreaming.

Her smile faded as a familiar voice nagged at her from inside her head. *Asleep or awake, it is still a sin.*

She lay down again and pulled the covers to her chin. She rolled over, trying to ignore the hum of her

body, the memory of his touch — she closed her eyes —
his devastating smile.

Chapter Three

"Hello, Mrs Gaitland!" Mr McElroy shouted above the din of customers.

Mr McElroy's general store buzzed with a swarm of customers. A wagon load of fresh fruit and vegetables had just arrived from Bisbee.

Beatrice smiled and waved a gloved hand at him from across the large cart. "Business is booming, I see."

"Indeed. Is there anything in particular you're looking for?"

"I have a list—" She waved a small piece of paper at him then shrugged as she wondered just how to get it to him.

He gestured to someone next to her. She turned to see who.

"Mrs Gaitland," Luke said with a slight bow. "Allow me."

Paying no attention to her heart, which had suddenly decided to try to jump out of her corset, she nodded and handed him the list. His fingers grazed her knitted gloves as he took it from her hand. She shivered under her shawl. Every time she looked into his eyes her insides turned molten, as they had the first time she'd noticed him.

She watched him out of the corner of her eye as he wove his way through the throng, reading her list, and handed it to Mr McElroy. Slowly she made her way to the cash stand. While Luke gathered her groceries, Mr McElroy tallied her list.

"I see you have a new helper, Mr McElroy." She nodded in Luke's direction.

"Yup, he's a hard worker so far, but, then again, they all start out that way then later on, end up asleep in the back."

"Well, not this one." She smiled. "I have a good feeling about him — about his work habits, I mean," Beatrice corrected unnecessarily. She turned away, hoping Mr McElroy hadn't noticed the heat in her cheeks.

Beatrice gathered an armload of tomatoes from the newly arrived items and turned back to the cash stand. "Oh, my. I'm going to need to borrow your wheelbarrow again, I fear, Mr McElroy. I've no way of getting all this home." She indicated with a tilt of her head to the two crates Luke had packed.

"Not to worry, Mrs Gaitland, I'll have Luke here help you home."

Her eyes flew to Luke's steady gaze.

"That'll be a dollar-fifty, Mrs Gaitland."

Mesmerised by the blue fire in Luke's eyes, she almost missed Mr McElroy's statement. "Of — of course." Hurriedly she brought her attention to her reticule. After handing Mr McElroy the coins, she and Luke set out.

Beatrice dared not speak until they were away from the main street of town, for anyone within hearing distance would be able to detect in her voice the longing she harboured for Luke.

She knew the odd ache she felt for him was totally irrational, but his soul held a beauty one could see in his eyes. Still... She shook herself mentally. This feeling must be quelled, and fast. Yearning for something could not call the situation into being, or deem it appropriate.

Desperate to be distracted from her feuding thoughts, she spoke. "Luke, you said you're not from here originally. What was it that brought you out West?" She stole a glance at him as she awaited his answer. He carried the two full crates. She'd insisted on taking the smaller bundle of vegetables.

She watched him jerk his chin as if in dismissal.

"Adventure, I guess. That and moving on to the next town seemed advisable at the time."

She worked up another question but he spoke first.

"Mrs Gaitland, are you making lemonade? You seem to have a wagon load of lemons here."

Unable to contain her smile, she answered. "Lemons are not only for consuming, you know."

He turned his head to look at her. "Enlighten me." He raised an eyebrow as if sceptical.

"I add the juice of lemons to the water when I wash my hair, and goat's milk and lemon for my skin. Lemon can also be used in laundry. It lends a bit more freshness to the water than just soap."

"Your vanity shall strip every lemon tree in Bisbee of its fruit," he said in that dry, teasing tone of his.

She laughed. Had anyone else uttered those words she would have been insulted. "Would you prefer I smelt like rancid animal fat and looked as spotted and old as a mountain crone?"

He smiled and adjusted the crates in his arms. "If you are referring to the faint sprinkling across your nose and cheeks, I happen to find it charming."

"Flatterer."

"Not at all. But worry not, I shall let you know if you begin to smell like rancid animal fat."

They approached her cottage, and she opened the door for him to bring the crates in. "And just how, tactfully, mind you, would you go about informing me of my offence to your sense of smell?"

Luke walked through the front doorway, easily found the kitchen, placed the crates on the counter, and turned back to face her. "Tactfully? No, no. I'd simply say"—he leaned close to her and spoke in low tones—"madam, you smell."

She chuckled while stripping off her gloves, holding back the flood of joviality she felt at their tête-à-tête and the intimacy it seemed to create. "No matter how rude you came off, I believe you *would* say it that way, Luke." She grinned knowingly at him.

He nodded once. "Can I help you put these away?" He indicated the groceries inside the crates.

"It is very kind of you to offer, but I can take it from here. Just allow me to—"

As she made to open her reticule, Luke stepped forward and placed his hand over the top of hers. She felt the shock between them and looked up at him, half startled, half in anticipation.

"Please, keep your coin. It was my pleasure assisting such a lovely lady." He took her hand in his. Lifting it to his lips, he inhaled through his nose and added, "Who doesn't smell like rancid animal fat."

She giggled. "You rogue." But, when his lips met her skin and lingered, her smile wavered. Collecting her wits she swallowed and gently took her hand back. "You'd better run along back to Mr McElroy's."

He flashed her that shy smile of his and, in the next instant, he shut the front door as he departed.

With her heart seemingly in her throat, Beatrice stepped into the parlour to watch through the lace curtains Luke's retreat. He walked with a casual gait down the dirt path then up the street. Pressing her hand to her chest, she closed her eyes, still feeling the invisible warm mark his lips had left. Until he'd kissed her hand, her skin had been cold — her whole world had been cold. Now, this young man had branded her with his mouth, and her entire body sweltered at the memory.

* * * *

Luke's kiss seemed to have lingered on her hand for the rest of the morning, and Beatrice felt as if she were walking in the clouds. She went about her chores singing merry tunes.

"Molly, do you love me, love as I love you? Tell me, by those ringlets, by those eyes of blue."

From the doorway of her kitchen, Allen joined in. *"'Molly, do you love me, love as I love you?'* How does the rest go, Beatrice?"

With a startled intake of breath, she snapped her gaze to his and her cheeks heated. He'd entered her cottage without announcement. Aside from the embarrassment of Allen waking in on her singing, it angered her that he felt so free with her person. Refusing to let her now sour mood show, she turned her face away from him. "I don't recall the rest of that one."

He shut the door behind him and from under her lashes she watched as he strolled towards her, invading what had been her sanctuary—up until he had decided to occupy an active role in her life.

"I didn't know you were familiar with Stephen Foster tunes." He came to a stop in front of her and she looked up.

"Everyone has heard of Stephen Foster." She waved a dismissing hand, struggling to keep a civil smile on her face.

Allen reached out and took a strand of her hair, which had fallen in front of her ear, between his fingers. "I just figured you only knew sacred songs, is all," he nearly whispered.

She laughed and hoped the sound wasn't nearly as stiff as her ears perceived it to be. Gently pulling away, she announced luncheon.

* * * *

It wasn't his manners that raised Beatrice's hackles, it was his company. She watched as he chewed his food, and listened while he made light conversation. He reminded her of Lindley, she realised with a start. She took a sip of tea to avoid coughing up the crumbs she'd inhaled.

"And so, I have decided to purchase the property adjacent to this one. You know, the old Frank place? I will begin establishing myself in the house, starting tomorrow."

Allen's statement brought her slamming back into the conversation. "You mean you won't be staying at the hotel any longer?"

"Only for about two more days or so, while things are set to my standards." Then he looked at her, angling his head slightly. "Aw, you've been worried I wasn't getting enough care, surrounded by all those strangers."

She quickly pulled a pretend smile across her closed lips. Afraid the absurdity of his words would push the hilarity of his assumption over the edge and it would escape in a fit of laughter, she hid it behind a quick sip of tea.

"My dear, darling Beatrice, aren't you just the sweetest thing? Now you can cook every meal for me, and never have to be worried about my being lonely again."

Her laughter would have stopped high and dry with his last statement.

"Er, Allen, I never thought to—"

"No, no. I know what you are thinking. But I have great plans for the place."

Allen couldn't have a single clue as to what she thought or felt. It occurred to her that he actually believed she was there to cook his meals. She took a breath and made to put an end to it right then and there when he spoke.

"I visited the new place this morning—you must have been in town."

Beatrice thought she'd detected a flash of suspicion in his eyes, but, before she could react, he continued.

"The man from the town lot commission said the old well out back just needs to be re-tapped." He didn't allow her to comment, but forged ahead. "I am planning a water pump in the kitchen, and I will be adding a small room off the bedroom, and installing a real, genuine claw-foot porcelain bathtub. Doesn't it sound heavenly?"

Unbelievable. Now he'll be asking me to come over and scrub his back. Something was going to have to be said about this—she was neither his cook nor his maid, nor would she ever aspire to be such for him. "It sounds like you will be very comfortable there." Not knowing what else to say at the moment, she made to rise and clean up when Allen placed his hand upon hers.

"I would like you to know you will be welcome there...any time you wish it."

Good God! Could he have just issued to me a subtle invitation to his bed? In pursuance of her purpose to remove herself from the table, and the sheer necessity of it after his last utterance, she stood, and slid her hand from his. She took up the dessert plates and turned for the basin of water, ignoring what Allen must have thought as an enticement, and leaving it to hang in the air between them. With any luck, it would disappear altogether.

"How very kind of you, dear brother-in-law." She'd emphasised the title—not loudly, but with a subtle intensity—hoping he'd understand her position on the matter. At the thought of Allen bedding her, she masked her shudder of revulsion with a few quick swishes of her fingers in the water.

After a moment, he also rose from the table. "I would like to take you to Nellie Cashmen's restaurant tonight and buy you supper. You know, to celebrate my moving into the neighbourhood permanently."

She set the dishes into the water. *Not because I've earned a night of reprieve from the ovens?* "I'm afraid I can't, Allen. I have a few Shepherd of the Hills families to visit." Since Lindley's death, it wasn't a consistent hobby of hers to make the visitations, but it would soon become one if this uncomfortable situation with Allen persisted.

Allen stepped over to her and took her by the shoulders, turning her to face him. "But it shouldn't take you very long, not if you start out right after you clean up here."

Loath to spend every free moment of her time with Allen Gaitland, she searched frantically for an excuse. She pivoted away from him, shaking her head. Mercifully, she felt his hands fall away. However, much to her annoyance, he continued his prodding.

"Come on now, say you'll have supper with me tonight."

Remembering her cause, she spun on her heel to face him. "Allen, I'm in mourning. I shouldn't be seen—"

"Nonsense. I am your brother-in-law. No one would think twice about you being out and about with myself in attendance."

She had no other choice but to refuse the outrageous invitation. "I'm sorry, Allen, I will not jeopardise my reputation, and the reputation of Shepherd of the Hills."

Allen pouted in the same way that Lindley used to when coercing her to do something she wasn't fond of doing. Like the time he'd talked her into moving out West.

"Next week, then."

"Next year," she countered.

"Now you're being cruel."

"No, I'm being sensible."

Allen stomped his foot on the floor like a spoilt child then sobered as if he'd found a reason she could not refute. "Beatrice," he drawled, "I am providing you with your allowance. Don't endanger that by denying me a simple thing like your company."

In Allen's voice, she detected a strange combination of warning and whining she was more than familiar with. Placing a hand on her stomach to squelch the queasiness of sour memories, she smiled—a tight-lipped, placating grin, the only kind she'd suffer for him. Being on her own for the past six months had brought, along with the loneliness, a thread of dignity she'd been lacking when she'd been married.

She raised her chin a notch. "I had no idea you'd attached strings to your kindness."

Allen stared at her, not being able to reply for a few moments. "Think about it, will you? For me?" He mimicked the puppy eyes again.

After a moment's pause, she answered. "We'll see."

"Good," he stated with vigour as if she'd said yes. "I'll come by after sundown tonight. You will be here, won't you?"

"There is nowhere else for me to go." She shook her head in frustration.

Allen smiled, quite satisfied, and departed from the cottage.

She collapsed into a chair. "Men."

Chapter Four

Worrying her bottom lip, she pressed her face to her pillow and squeezed her eyes shut. She'd returned to her cottage after the visits, hastily extinguished the lamps, pulled every curtain over her windows, bolted her front and back doors, and climbed into bed as fast as she could. With any luck, when Allen knocked on her door, the dark stillness would discourage him from forcing her into a public appearance with him.

The sun had set no less than half an hour ago, but she knew for certain that Allen would come to call. She didn't need supper anyway. She had accepted tea and some edibles during her visits, and could now count her hunger sufficiently satisfied — another reason not to join her brother-in-law.

Hearing a light tapping on her front door, she held her breath.

"Beatrice? Are you home yet?"

It was Allen. An image of him skulking about her porch and peering into her windows flashed before her. She cringed then shilly-shallied with whether or not to answer.

The knock came a bit louder this time, accompanied by the jiggling of her front doorknob.

She sat up. Should she just answer and cry off, saying she was too tired or sick to go with him? Or would he insist and drag her into town, something Lindley would've not thought twice about doing?

When no other noises were heard, save the distant boom of thunder from somewhere out in the desert, she slid back under her covers, pulling them to her chin.

He'd gone, and somehow she knew he wouldn't be back. At least, not tonight.

Enveloped by a feeling of safety, she rolled over on to her side, taking the covers with her. She took a deep breath and sighed, whispering a prayer of thanks that she'd been spared Allen's blatant attempt at defaming her character.

She shoved every last thought of Allen to the back of her mind and relived the magic moment when Luke had kissed her hand that morning. After the sixth time or so, she drifted off to sleep, smiling and comforted to her toes.

* * * *

Thirsty, Beatrice headed towards the kitchen just before sunrise and spotted a letter that had been slipped under her front door. Picking it up and breaking the seal she saw that it was from Allen.

Apparently, he expected an answer as to where she'd been the night before.

She sighed. Did he really think she would be intimidated by his demands? She shook her head and read on. He informed her that he would be gone for most of the day running errands, then it was off to Bisbee for him.

She crushed the note in her palm and tossed the message into her fireplace where it fell behind the kindling. She wasn't under any obligation to Allen Gaitland, and he would have to come to terms with the fact sooner or later.

Beatrice paused. The whisper of a fresh type of independence hugged her like a new woollen shawl. In the kitchen she poured herself a drink of cool water from a ceramic pitcher, taking pleasure in the small respite from her duties. With a bounce in her step she returned to her room and crawled under the covers, not caring if she missed the breakfast hour or not. She wouldn't be sought after to cook two whole meals for Allen that day, all three if God would smile upon her.

* * * *

"Ah, Pastor Allen, good morning."

"The same to you, Mr McElroy."

"What brings you into town so bright and early today?"

"Well, I have purchased the old Frank place and it needs some care, as you would imagine, having stood abandoned and exposed to the weather conditions these many months."

"I see. What are you interested in?"

"For starters, a good whitewash."

"I have just the one. Will you be doing this yourself, then?"

He grinned. "No, no. I'm afraid I lack the talent." When Mr McElroy bobbed his head as if he understood, Allen continued. "In addition, I hoped to enquire about a few hands to clear the weeds, and, most of all, re-tap the water well."

"I see. Well, you are welcome to borrow my new lad, Luke, for a few days, but for the well-tappers I'd want to send out for someone familiar with the process."

Allen nodded. "I'd be much obliged, Mr McElroy."

Mr McElroy disappeared into the back room. Shortly thereafter, his new employee emerged and introduced himself.

"I'm Luke. I understand you have some work for me?"

Allen smiled, but cast a visual assessment that flashed from Luke's head to his boots and back again. He'd seen this boy before — prowling around Beatrice like a cat on heat while she fed slop to the pigs of this sad little mining camp. "I do. I am Pastor Allen." He nodded in Luke's direction.

Luke nodded back and his gaming instincts leapt to attention. He knew exactly who this snake was — he'd recognised him from Stone Soup Hour and didn't trust him, not as far as he could kick him. Around the gambling tables across America and its territories, he'd observed 'Pastor' Allen's kind. They appeared in public to be straight-laced and starch-cuffed, but underneath they were a bunch of sharpers and blacklegs. Not that this particular man frequented the gaming halls, but he was easier to read than a novice with a deck of marked cards. And he didn't like the way he acted all high and mighty around Mrs Gaitland — as if she were his lapdog.

"Walk the property with me and I can show you what needs to be accomplished."

"If I am qualified to do the jobs, I'm your man." He nodded and took up his hat from a peg in the wall.

Luke followed him out of the door with every intention to convince 'Pastor' Allen of his lack of skill and interest in domestic chores.

* * * *

By the length of the shadows, it was nearly nine in the morning when Luke arrived with several buckets of whitewash and garden tools. Acutely aware of Mrs Gaitland's presence not two hundred feet from where he was, he began his chores. Her proximity was, after all, the only reason he'd taken the job.

He'd whitewashed the whole of the porch area when the well-tappers arrived, and by the time he'd made his way around the entire house, he heard they'd broken through the rock to a water source that was not subject to seasonal variations of rainfall.

After the tappers had taken up their tools and left, Luke turned to see Beatrice puttering around in her garden.

"Howdy, Mrs Gaitland," Luke called out to her as he approached.

She looked up and smiled. "Hello, Luke. You've had a busy day, I see."

Beatrice watched as he looked at his work then slid her a shy smile. He shrugged a shoulder. "Guess so."

If she wasn't so upset about her garden, her stomach would have done a little flip at that grin of his. She glanced down at the result of her toiling.

"What's that—are you sporting a frown, Mrs Gaitland?"

Timidly she met his gaze. "Oh, it's nothing really. I'm just lamenting over my poor garden. It seems the *varmints* around here are benefiting from all my hard work."

"That they are." Luke indicated to the house behind him with a tilt of his head and a grin.

Her lips twitched. Was it possible that Luke knew about Allen using her as his cook?

Luke walked over and stood across the garden from her. "Have you thought about setting up a scarecrow to intimidate the critters?"

She felt her body relax, but could it have been the man himself or merely his suggestion that had eased her? "No, I had not. What a brilliant idea."

He shrugged a shoulder. "I'd be glad to help you, if you want."

"Thank you, Luke. Let me get a few things from inside."

Some minutes later, she returned, not only with an outfit and stuffing for the scarecrow, but also with two tall glasses of lemonade. Setting the things down, she waved him over to the shade of her porch and handed Luke his glass. "I felt guilty about what you said the other day, so I took most of the lemons and used them for consumption purposes."

Luke took a sip of his drink and flashed her another shy smile. "I didn't mean for you to feel badly, I was merely teasing."

"I know, but you really made me think. Besides, if I can get the local animals to stop gnawing on the leaves of my little patch, I may be able to provide my own lemons. That" — she indicated with a salute of her glass to a near-bare branch poking out of the ground — "will be a lemon tree someday, with any luck."

He took another drink. "Good, because your lemonade is as delicious as your stew. Have you ever thought about opening a restaurant?"

She giggled and waved away the notion. After taking a few gulps of her drink, she then set it down and scooped up the clothes for the scarecrow.

Luke put his glass next to hers. "Here, allow me." He took the plaid flannel shirt from her and held it up against his chest, buttons towards her.

With determination she began unfastening the shirt, ignoring the jolt that shot through her at the feeling of his warm hard chest beneath the soft fabric. She glanced up at his face and found him smirking. She quickly returned her attention to the shirt front.

"What?" she asked, smiling, affected by his unexpected grin.

"Nothing," he replied, and, after a moment, "I envy the man whose chest was bared under the ministrations of your nimble fingers," he all but whispered.

She snapped her gaze to his eyes and she laughed, shrugging off his comment and purposefully disregarding the intense heat of his stare. "Out of decorum, I shall ignore your mischievous remark, young man."

"Do as you will. However, I shall revisit the idea when I lay me down to sleep tonight."

Having popped open the last button, she took the shirt from him and laid it upon the ground. When she picked up the trousers, Luke made to take them from her. She pulled them out of his reach.

"I don't think so," she said, unable to keep her voice from dipping low with seductive mirth.

He gave her one of those smiles again, which, despite the warmth of the day, sent gooseflesh spreading from her shoulders and down her back.

With some scrap wood, Luke fashioned a cross for the scarecrow. While Beatrice dressed the cross and stuffed the clothes with rags, Luke dug the hole for the post.

Luke set the mock farmer up and they stood back to admire their work.

"Well done, Mrs Gaitland."

She set the straw hat on top of the post and secured it with an old length of ribbon.

Shrugging a shoulder, she spoke. "I suppose it's a little late to try and save the plants, but keeping a garden gives me something to do other than church work. I should feel guilty —"

"Why? You're not a nun, you know." He tossed his hat to the ground, took a piece of cloth from the pile of rags and draped it over his hair. "Hello, I'm Sister Gaitland," he said in falsetto and paused as if waiting for a reaction from her. When she smiled, he continued. "I am married to the church. I have no need for the touch of a man."

"Now, stop your teasing, Luke." She chuckled. "I've always hated being laughed at," she murmured with a mock pout, dismissing his last comment.

"Oh, so I've found a sore spot, have I?" he taunted, letting the fabric slip from his head and taking up his hat once again.

"Not in the least." She looked away.

Luke reached over and, with a knuckle, nudged her chin so that she had no choice but to look at him. His eyes were suddenly very serious. With a gentle hand he took her by the jaw, his thumb idly stroking her cheek. "Then answer the question."

"You did not ask me a question," she uttered, then swallowed nervously.

"No, I did not. But a question hangs in the air as to whether or not you have the need for a man's touch."

A few heartbeats went by, louder than the soft breeze rushing past her ears. Beatrice attempted to pull out of his hand. "We shouldn't be speaking of—"

"Then your answer is clear. You *are* in need of a man's touch."

Breaking free of his light hold, she swept off her hands. "I have finished for the day. Thank you for your help." After a few steps, she broke into a run to the porch. Her instincts told her he followed close behind.

Just as she'd suspected, Luke caught up with her. He swung her around by the arm. His grip wasn't hurtful, but insistent. "You don't have to be afraid of me, Mrs Gaitland."

"Nonsense, I'm not afraid—"

"Yes, you are." Luke took a step closer to her, causing her to take a step backward.

Beatrice flinched when her bottom met the door behind her. "No, I'm not."

"Then prove it."

Somehow, he'd inched even closer. The fabric of their clothes seemed to heat up as if the sun had allowed a beam of light to form in the non-existent space between them.

"Prove it, how?" Her voice was laced with sincere incredulity. She watched as Luke's lips curled up at the corners.

"Let me kiss you."

She hoped to God he hadn't heard her breath catch in her throat. She attempted to divert his attention from the sound with a shake of her head "I don't think it would be appropriate."

"So, you are frightened of me, of the magnetism between us."

Beatrice squirmed against him, attempting to escape their close proximity. "Don't be silly. I am in mourning, as you already know."

On either side of Beatrice's shoulders, Luke raised his hands to rest on the door behind her. "And, if we were in the middle of the street, I'd be inclined to follow the stringent rules of your mourning period. But, as it is, we are alone on your back porch."

"Luke, please," she whispered breathlessly.

Luke's gaze slid to her lips. "Just one kiss, Mrs Gaitland." His face moved closer to hers. "One long, tender kiss."

Chapter Five

She could feel their breath mingling, his chest pressed against hers, his warmth penetrating through to her very bones. She opened her mouth to reply and his lips touched hers, soft and sweet. The intoxicating mix of his body weight and undemanding mouth triggered Beatrice's eyes to languidly close. Fourth of July fireworks exploded in jubilation behind her eyelids. It was, without a doubt, the most stirring kiss she'd ever experienced.

Her body reacted, her back arching, causing her chest to press harder into his. When he groaned and deepened the kiss, she made to slide her arms around his neck, but, from inside the cottage, just on the other side of the door they leaned against, she heard Allen calling her name. With a gasp, she pushed away from Luke and took a few steps to the other side of the porch, just as the door opened.

"Ah, there you are. Where were you last night? I came—" Allen turned his head, unsuccessfully hiding his surprise at seeing Luke there upon the porch with her. "So, have you finished my improvements already, young man?"

Luke eyed his temporary employer coolly, his feathers not appearing to be ruffled at all by the sudden appearance of Allen. "Tomorrow I'll do a few more touch-ups on the whitewash. Afterwards I'll take care of the weeds then all will be complete."

"Ah, good." He grinned like a snake. "So what are we doing now?"

"Mrs Gaitland and I were just admiring our handiwork." He indicated to the scarecrow stuck in the ground in the midst of the tilled soil rows and nibbled-upon greens. "What do you think, Pastor Allen?"

Allen barely glanced at the scarecrow, his attention instead falling on Beatrice. "Are you well, my dear?"

Beatrice's gaze flew from the mock farmer to Allen's, longing to drive him and his suspicions out into the dessert. "I am. I—I suppose I've had too much sun today."

Allen's eyes narrowed, but he blinked and the tension seemed to slip away. "Well, I'm sure Luke here has other things to attend to. Why don't you go into the house and start supper. I'd like to see what he has accomplished today." He opened the door for her to step through.

Without sparing even a courteous glance to either gentleman, she turned and went inside.

* * * *

After Luke had shown Allen all he'd done to the old house, Allen dismissed him, but not without a final word or two. "By the way, in case you have your sights set on the widow Gaitland, you need to know something. It was her late husband's desire that I take his place in more ways than just the ministry at Shepherd of the Hills"—he grinned—"and I have every intention of fulfilling his wishes."

"I believe Mrs Gaitland will have a say in that, especially since we are not in medieval England."

Allen looked Luke up and down with a wry smile upon his lips. "What do you know of medieval England? You are an uneducated field hand."

Luke removed his hat and bowed to Allen with a flourish. "*Good night, sweet prince: And flights of angels sing thee to thy rest.*"

Allen laughed with superiority. "From what medieval manuscript is that?"

Luke righted his hat. "It wasn't from a medieval manuscript, but from *Hamlet* by William Shakespeare, who is a somewhat famous Elizabethan playwright." He touched the brim in a farewell gesture, turned on his heel, and left Allen standing there trying his best to look aloof.

"What an ass," Luke murmured to himself.

* * * *

Relief flooded Beatrice when Allen left after supper. She was even more grateful that he hadn't reintroduced the topic of the scene on the back porch. As she dried the dishes and put them away, she finally allowed herself to dwell on Luke's kiss.

The touch of his lips on hers had mesmerised her. His evident masculinity had held her hostage—he'd simply consumed her when he'd pushed her up against that back door. It made her feel utterly feminine, even desired—desired in a raw, sensual way totally foreign to her. Oh, what she wouldn't do to be free of her bereavement period and encourage such actions and more with that blue-eyed devil. The red-orange glow in her soul that began on the first night Luke had spoken to her was now beginning to leap with dangerous flames.

She heaved a sigh, hoping to cool her heated flesh.

If he'd only come to Tombstone after her bereavement, she would have gladly allowed him to –

Beatrice caught herself. *What am I thinking?* She could never disregard her status in town in favour of her own carnal desires. It would be very selfish. Perhaps she should just discourage Luke from any more advances. But how? It wasn't as if she were soliciting his attentions.

But allowing him to be so forward was almost like egging him on, wasn't it?

After washing and crawling into bed, Beatrice imagined how it would be had they met in more favourable circumstances. Tonight she let the fantasy run where it would, even unto the point of Luke lifting her nightdress and making love to her. She imagined her wifely duties and pictured Luke's face instead of Lindley's. Luke would probably kiss her and put his hands on her, not just because he *had* to – to move her nightgown aside – but because he *wanted* to. He'd touch her legs, her hips, the small of her back. He'd whisper pretty things into her ear, and it would tickle, so that she'd get all goosepimply like she was right now.

Beatrice fell asleep with an unprecedented desire burning in her bosom.

* * * *

Luke lay upon his bedroll thinking of his young widow, as he had for the last — who knew how long? It had seemed like forever. There'd been nothing before in his mind that had taken up his thoughts the way she did.

Earlier in the day, before they'd made the scarecrow, all Luke had been able to concentrate on was the sounds coming from the Gaitland place.

While she'd been about her business inside, he'd heard her whistling. The thought of her luscious lips puckered as she'd done so had nearly driven Luke to distraction. He'd felt dizzy as he'd imagined those soft lips drawing on his prick.

Every once in a while, a verse or a chorus had floated on the air to where he'd stood, trying to look interested in anything other than the goings-on in his head. Her voice was clear and feminine, and all he could think about was her singing his name as he took her hard and long. Hell, he'd walked around with his cock like a brick in his pants for most of the morning.

Luke knew the kiss they'd shared on her back porch hadn't frightened her off — her tenacity proved her strength — and their attraction would only become intensified because of her spirit. She might go so far as to shy away from him for a little while, but not so much as to ignore him. Her sense of courtesy would overrule her temporary timidity, of this he was certain.

Luke smiled as he remembered her wide eyes as he'd closed in for their kiss, and her lips that had so willingly returned his attentions, her body that had risen and pressed itself against his. Luke knew down deep she could be enticed to allow him all manner of liberties. The passionate nature he'd sensed within her would take precedence over the ridiculous societal rules she'd been following. Had they been allowed to finish their kiss he would have held her soft body against his until she'd melted in his arms.

He swore. For the next couple of days he would be tortured by the nearness of the hauntingly familiar widow Gaitland. He was sure to run mad if he didn't have her soon.

＊ ＊ ＊ ＊

Beatrice woke to the sound of a pick slamming into the earth. Frowning, she wandered over to a window and there was Luke, hoeing the soil next to the old Frank place—Allen's new place, she corrected herself.

She let her breath out slowly at the sight before her.

He'd removed his shirt and she refused to take her eyes from his rippling physique. Not that he looked huge and beefy, like on a poster of the Strong Man from the circus, but he was indeed manly. His powerful-looking shoulders were rounded, and, moreover, the muscles of his arms curved in and out underneath tanned skin. But it was his waist that caused her pulse to jump—taut down the sides and rippled in front like a thick washboard. *I could think of a few things to rinse out, had I access to his equipment.* With wide eyes, Beatrice abruptly turned from the window. Where on earth had that lustful thought come from? Mercy, she'd never even heard things of that nature before!

She lifted her fingers and plied them to her tense temples. She remembered the kiss he'd given her as his body had pressed into hers against the door of her back porch. She'd practically turned into someone else entirely after that one glorious moment.

She found it impossible to ignore Luke as he worked away outside. She turned back to face the window and watched as he pulled the weeds he'd been loosening in the soil.

When all of the unwanted wild plants were in a pile, she realised she'd been there watching him for nearly two hours.

Wiping her damp hands on her chemise, she drew a deep breath into her lungs and stepped away from the window. Beatrice knew she needed to get away and not stare at him for the rest of the day. She went about dressing herself in a hand-me-down mourning gown and old hoop set, and made plans to attend to the patches of greenery and flowers she'd planted around the Shepherd of the Hills tent.

Very quietly, she slipped on to her back porch, grabbed her watering can, and took it into the house. Taking up a bonnet of faded black cotton, she darted out of her front door, so as not to be spotted by Luke, and headed towards the church's meeting tent.

* * * *

It hadn't taken Beatrice too many trips to the creek and back until the plants were sufficiently watered. She set down the watering can and untied a flap in the tent, tacking it open with the ties. She felt her shoulders relax as the cool darkness beckoned to her. Pulled in by some unknown force, she stepped in and sat in the first row, the very place she'd occupied during Lindley's many sermons. She removed her bonnet and began to pray.

"I'm not really certain why I'm here. Perhaps I just need reassurance." *Maybe even permission,* she added silently. But permission from whom? God? Lindley?

"Anyone who will listen," she whispered then laughed, the hollow sound bouncing around inside the near-empty tent. She'd needed to ask Lindley's permission for *everything* during the years they'd been married, why not now?

She sighed and closed her eyes. Her thoughts had not been anywhere near pure lately, and she felt horribly guilty about it. It was as if her flesh had decided to take over where her spiritual inclinations had once been.

Lindley would have told her Satan was to blame. She'd heard her husband's sermons enough times to have them ingrained into her very being. He would also have told her to repent her evil ways, and turn to a clean and spiritually purified way of life.

But it wasn't fair. She'd not sought another man's attentions. In fact, she'd rejected the advances of both Luke *and* Allen.

"All right," she admitted after a moment of contemplation. She had not been attracted to Allen, as she was to Luke. Allen did nothing but repel her, and Luke — Luke heated her blood to liquid silver. Beatrice relaxed and her head tilted back at the very idea of his hands —

"Kind of dark in here for a church," Luke's voice teased from the entrance flap.

She wasn't even startled. In fact, she'd half expected him to show up.

"May I join you?"

She turned to him. "Yes," she replied in near-whispered tones. She was thankful he'd donned his shirt before seeking her out.

He sat on the bench behind her and she turned to face him. He cleared his throat. "I know you must think I'm crazy, but I truly can't help but think we've met before."

Beatrice looked down at her folded hands, resting in her lap. "You are not crazy. I must look like someone you know, that's all."

"I wish it were as simple as you insinuate." He chuckled. "Let me ask you this—have you ever been to Dodge City?"

She looked up at his expectant face and shook her head. "No, I haven't."

"How about New Orleans?"

"I'm afraid not."

Luke took a breath as if to offer another possible town but clamped his mouth shut. He shook his head and rolled his eyes. "If I sat here and named every town, city and gambling hall I've ever visited, you *would* call me crazy."

"If you were to start naming gambling halls to a woman who used to be a preacher's wife, thinking she'd even stepped foot into an establishment of that ilk, I'd have to concur."

Both she and Luke laughed.

"I suppose you are right," he murmured, accompanied by his shy smile, which never failed to curl her toes.

At once they stood. Someone was whistling a tune and the song was increasing in volume as the person approached the entrance to the tent.

"It's Allen," Beatrice whispered quickly and snatched up her bonnet. "My late husband used to know that particular tune." The thought flitted through her mind again of how similar they were, but she had bigger problems in her immediate future.

She watched as Luke looked around frantically. It would be impossible to reach another flap and untie it in time to escape. She was trapped. *They* were trapped. *Together*.

The moment Beatrice turned towards the entrance to welcome Allen, Luke dived under her hoops.

"Allen," Beatrice squeaked. She cleared her throat. "What are you doing here?"

"I've come to rehearse my sermon for next week. Why is it so dark in here?"

She shrugged and watched as Allen went around untying every flap until the light and heat of the afternoon replaced the coolness of the once-dark tent.

"Did you wish to watch? I wouldn't mind the audience."

When she made to answer, Luke's hands settled on her ankles. She coughed. Loudly. "No." She shook her head, practically wadding up the bonnet in her fist. "No, no. I must go now." Very slowly, she took a sidestep. "I have watered the plants around the tent." She took a few more short steps in the direction of the entrance, and, when she paused, Luke's hands slid over her calves to the backs of her knees. "They are no longer thirsty." She angled her head and smiled woodenly, taking a few more steps towards freedom. "They will be nice and green by Sunday." Good God, his hands were slowly moving up her thighs.

"Are you well?" Allen studied her from behind the pulpit.

"I feel fine, just fine."

"You do indeed," came the barely audible voice from under her skirts.

She covered her bark of laughter with another cough. "I have to go now. Please don't forget to close up when you are finished."

Her intake of breath happened as Luke's hands cupped her bottom. She turned to bolt when Allen's voice stopped her flight.

"Just a moment."

"Yes?" she asked innocently, craning her neck to look at him, feeling Luke's hands gently massaging her seat. When Allen looked her up and down, she felt sure he knew someone was hiding under her skirts. Her knees would have buckled, had Allen not been scrutinising her person.

"I think..." He paused.

She held her breath.

"Rabbit for dinner would suit me."

Nearly falling over, partially from relief and the rest from her knees turning to water over what felt like kisses through her bloomers on the backs of her thighs, she exhaled. "Yes, rabbit. Done. Well, bye." She waved the wad of cloth that had once been her bonnet, then began her slow descent en route to the creek.

Once positive they could no longer be seen from the tent, she raised her hoops and kicked at Luke.

"I have changed my mind, you *are* crazy!" She threw the ruined bonnet at him and it bounced off harmlessly.

Luke fell over onto the grass, laughing. "You should have heard your voice, it must have gone up four octaves!" He held his stomach as he rolled on the ground.

She wanted so badly to be mad at him, but, truly, he had caused no physical damage. And, because of his ingenuity, they had not been caught together. She still felt he needed a reprimand, though. "Do you know the trouble I would've gotten into had you been discovered under my skirts?" She glared at him while he tried hard to control his mirth.

"I'm sorry," he spoke sincerely as he smiled. "Truly, I had no other option—"

She raised her hands. "Enough." She pressed her lips together to avoid breaking out in impending giggles.

Luke stood. Looking her in the eye, he pointed at her lips. "I see that smile on your face," he teased in a sing-song voice.

She closed her eyes and felt it impossible not to express amusement. "All right, you have me." She grinned, chuckling.

Luke grabbed her by the waist and hoisted her into the air. "Ah-ha! I knew I could make you laugh!"

"You cur, put me down." She giggled in opposition of her words. Once her feet were on the ground, she sobered and admonished him. "Don't you ever do that again!" She wagged a motherly finger at him. "And you keep your hands to yourself, young man!" Beatrice would have sworn she could still feel his touch.

"Can I make it up to you?"

"How on earth could you do so?"

Luke sobered. "I will help you catch a rabbit for your supper."

She groaned. "Oh, I had forgotten his request. He may as well have asked for lobster."

Luke chuckled. "Well, I can't help you with seafood, but rabbit I can do." He held out his hand to her. "Come."

* * * *

About a mile and a half from the Shepherd of the Hills tent, Luke and Mrs Gaitland sat in a field of tall grass, speaking softly about the hot, dry weather and odd things they noticed about the world around them. Luke had set the rabbit trap just inside a thin copse of cottonwood trees to the north, not a stone's pitch away.

He'd have bet a stack of ten-dollar chips he would have remembered by now where he'd seen her before, but as the days progressed he'd become more and more impatient with his faulty memory.

"Mrs Gaitland, look at me," he insisted, trying not to touch her — to pull her to him and demand she tell him why he continually drew blank cards on this subject.

She looked, but raised a sceptical eyebrow over a thickly lashed, dark brown eye. "Just what do you have planned when I do so, Luke?"

Impressed by her boldness and at the same time hoping she wouldn't shy away from their intimate tête-à-tête, Luke shook his head. "No, it's nothing like that. I just — well, I'm positive I know you from somewhere." He took a moment and studied her. Searching from the top of her head to her lips he strove to get his memory to jog.

"Ha!" She turned from him. "I think you are going to trap me into another kiss. Well, I'm not going to fall for your trickery ever again."

Luke mostly suppressed his grin. *So kissing was on her mind, was it?* "I don't need tricks to get you to kiss me." He spoke matter-of-factly, challenging her to investigate further.

"Yes, you do," was all she afforded him.

"How do you figure?"

Mrs Gaitland was thoughtful for a moment. "I've already told you. I am in mourning, and there is no polite way, rational reason, or anything else I can think of, which could cause you to make me do such. So the only munitions you have left are your ploys." She jerked her chin away to gaze out over the prairie.

"A very logical argument. However—" Luke paused.

She turned back to him. "However what?"

"Your reasoning is slightly skewed."

"It is not."

"Indeed, it is. You have all these arguments against kissing me—and all of them have to do with what *other* people think."

"There's nothing wrong with being concerned about one's reputation."

"No. Nevertheless, there is no one here to pass judgement." With a sweep of his hand he indicated to the field in which they sat.

She froze, ensnared by her own words.

"Therefore, Mrs Gaitland, there would be no harm whatsoever in a kiss."

She knelt before him, her cheeks flushed and oh-so-fetching. "I would know! Doesn't my opinion count for something?"

Luke nodded. "Indeed it does."

She let out a breath, her annoyance deflated by his agreement.

"On the other hand," he drawled, "if you had another not-so-flimsy excuse, say, perhaps you didn't like my kiss or you were not attracted to me, I'd be more inclined to concede."

Her eyes widened, but she uttered not one word—which pleased him greatly.

"So you see I *could* kiss you, no tricks, ploys or cons needed."

"That's absurd."

Luke rose up on his knees directly in front of her and pulled her to him like he'd been dying to do since they'd sat down. "No," he denied. "Far from it." And he lowered his face to hers.

Chapter Six

Damnation! He's done it again! But, oh, how wonderful his lips are. Suddenly, Beatrice gripped Luke's hard shoulder with one hand and snaked her other arm about his waist. She could feel the heat of the taut muscles of his torso from underneath his shirt. She sighed, and not a heartbeat later he coaxed her mouth open, sweeping his tongue over hers. The ground seemed to tilt, but his arms tightened around her, steadying her confused equilibrium.

She felt Luke's hand at the nape of her neck — the other caressed her lower back, dipping below the bottom edge of her corset to graze the top of her buttocks through the fabric of her skirts. Consumed by lust, or passion, or some breeding of the two emotions she couldn't name, her body went from hosting tiny sparks to a full-blown funeral pyre. She needed more oxygen before she fainted in earnest. Turning her head to the side, she broke out of his kiss.

They held on to one another, panting as if they'd just sprinted up a steep hill.

Beatrice attempted to calm her racing heart. She let her hands fall to her sides as rational thought came back. "Luke, we mustn't do this."

"I know." His lips swept over her temple. "But denying myself is more painful than the fabricated shame you guard so fiercely."

She tried to pull away.

After placing his lips on her cheek for one more kiss, he let her go.

"My shame is real." He made to protest but she continued. "We can only be friends, Luke. You mustn't kiss me anymore. It's not right."

"It might not be right for society, but it feels right to me."

Just then she heard the trap catch.

Leaving their argument in the field, they went to see what Luke had caught.

"Two rabbits!" she exclaimed. "How on earth did you do that?"

Luke lifted the rope and two good-sized rabbits squirmed from the loop in the end. "Jacks, and both of them look healthy. I'll bet they're the varmints who've been gratifying themselves in your garden."

"You could very well be correct," she murmured as a vision of her garden being ravaged by the critters flashed before her.

Luke nodded. "M-hm." He lifted them to eye level. "Justice will be served, and then dinner. In that order," he said to the rabbits as if they could understand.

She smiled then sobered. "Um, I've never actually killed before I cook," she confessed, avoiding the eyes of her dinner.

Luke smiled. "Count it as all part of my contrition. I'll do it for you."

"My hero," she stated in contradiction of her churning emotions, amazed that the words hadn't passed over her lips with a heartfelt, heroine-like sigh. Indeed she might accidentally let one slip next time if she didn't stop fantasising about him. And he really needed to stop kissing her. It was imperative to her sanity.

* * * *

Luke had prepared the rabbit meat without her having to witness, and for that she was thankful. She was also thankful that Luke hadn't tried to kiss her again before he'd departed. She'd been attempting to convince herself for the tenth time since they'd left the field that they really shouldn't do that anymore.

"And how is my little cook doing this evening?" Allen joked as he entered her kitchen.

She had just finished setting the table and was not amused at all by his dubbing her 'his little cook'.

"Allen, it's not right for you to enter my cottage unannounced."

"But, Beatrice, your door was unlocked—"

"An unlocked door doesn't give you the right to just walk in," she interrupted, not wishing for an argument, but for an acceptance of her wishes.

He waved a hand, dismissing the subject, and sat down at the table.

Allowing a frustrated breath to escape, she continued her discourse. "And I'm positive I don't like to be called your cook."

"Were you able to get rabbit for supper?" He smiled, his puppy-dog eyes foolishly attempting to melt her ire.

He'd changed the subject without so much as a pause.

She turned away to check the meat. "I was," she murmured then clenched her jaw shut.

When supper was over, Allen patted his belly, a subtle approval, she surmised.

He sighed. "Did the hotel help you out with the meal? It sure was good."

Beatrice tried not to glare at Allen. *Does he think I couldn't have come up with the recipe on my own?* "Allen—"

"I know, I know. I should not have called you my cook earlier. I'm sorry."

She made to reply but he continued. "I actually have another little project for you, which has nothing to do with cooking."

"What is it?" Her scepticism rung true in her question. After all, what other choice did she have? He provided her with food—and now he offered to relieve her enforced domesticity.

He wadded up his linen napkin and set it atop his plate. "The improvements are just about finished on the property I purchased. I was hoping you would be inclined to obtain a few items for me. You know—curtains, dishes, pots and pans, linens and the like. I will also need furniture, a bed, a wardrobe, and the bathtub, of course." He smiled. "I need you to give the place a woman's touch."

"I see. And what is your budget for all of these grand, new items?"

"Don't you worry your pretty little head over it. You can spend as much as you need."

At once she felt as if she were in her parents' home again. She'd not gone on a shopping spree in years. "Truly?" she asked, breathless at the thought. An occupation was sure to relieve the tediousness of her situation—and perhaps he wouldn't pay such close attention to her personal life.

"I wouldn't want anyone else to do it." He grinned at her.

"What colours were you—"

Allen reached across the table and took her hand. "You choose. I trust your judgement."

Beatrice smiled back, excitement bubbling up inside her. She was thrilled with the prospect of doing something other than merely existing. "I'll start tomorrow."

* * * *

Allen walked back to the hotel whistling a merry tune, his hands fisted into balls hidden deep in his pockets in contrast. Every time he saw his brother's widow, she looked more and more alluring—God, how he wanted to poke her. He'd have to slake his more carnal desires with a whore again, as he'd had to just about every other night. But he wasn't entirely discouraged about the future. After Beatrice's little shopping extravaganza, she would be more charmed than ever with him, he mused. Not only was he fulfilling every woman's dream of having no budget when shopping, but she would see all of his new items and long to move in with him—another, more enticing boon.

All of his life he'd lived in the shadow of Lindley, his father's *first-born son*. God, how many times had he heard that phrase uttered by his parents—as if announcing royalty had arrived into town. The brat had seemed to get everything he'd wanted—from that stupid hoop game Allen so coveted in their youth, to every girl Allen had ever looked sideways at. Even at school, his big brother had been lauded as the cleverest boy ever to graduate from the small town's one-room schoolhouse. Things, people and even money, had been handed to Lindley on a silver tray.

Until now.

How ironic that whatever riches or social connections Lindley had taken a lifetime to accumulate were now Allen's—and with very little effort on his part.

He grinned, holding in check the humour of it all. Lindley had to have been the worst charlatan in the history of the church. He'd hoarded every penny his congregation had bestowed upon him, never building a proper house of God, but tucking the tithes away in a bank account in his own name. A pity for Lindley that he'd never appreciated his end would come so soon, and that he couldn't have taken his earthly treasures with him when he went to meet the maker whose name he'd tossed around so lightly.

And to think Beatrice would never know it was Lindley's money she'd be spending to furnish her brother-in-law's, or, should he say, *future husband's* abode.

* * * *

By the light of a few hanging oil lamps, Luke sat at a rickety table in the corner of a tent saloon on the edge of town, his fingers itching with the need to play a hand of cards. He hadn't played in what seemed like months, and had come out tonight looking for a bit of social interaction in the form of a card game.

As aching as his body had been for a good tumble lately, he'd waved off a handful of scarlet ladies. That sort of exercise was not what he wanted tonight—at least, not from any of them. Only the sweet Mrs Gaitland could satisfy him, the woman he couldn't get out of his head, his wide-awake fantasies and the dreams he'd woken up from soaked in sweat and hard as a petrified oak.

He glanced across the tent at the available doves. *Perhaps if they were cleaner, less hair on their faces, more teeth in their mouths.* He sighed.

A pair of smiling brown eyes floated though his mind.

Then again, maybe not.

Luke sat with his near-empty beer mug when a familiar face stepped up to the makeshift bar of wooden planks and stacked barrels. Luke sat up straighter to get a better look. The man glanced over at the squeak of his chair.

The bartender set before the newcomer a shot of what must have been whisky, but his customer was far from satisfied. "I'll take the bottle, unless you think one of these other *fine* customers has enough silver to buy it from you," he drawled in a Georgian accent and swept his hand in an arch, indicating to the sorry lot that made up the few patrons of this particular establishment.

The barkeep pulled a face and handed him the bottle.

"Thank ya kindly," the customer said in the direction of the bartender, flipped him a coin then cleared his lungs of something thick, moist and most likely foul.

Luke watched as the man tossed back the shot then turned to approach him, his smile widening as he drew closer.

"Good to see you again, Doc." Luke waited until the whisky bottle and empty glass had been set upon the table before reaching out to shake the man's hand.

"Well, this is about as lost as you can get." He shook Luke's hand warmly.

"You did say to lose myself, didn't you?"

"Yeah, but I didn't think you'd crawl this close to the gapin' mouth o' Hell."

Luke chuckled. "It isn't quite *that* bad." Luke indicated the chair. "Have a seat." He watched Doc settle in. "You just get into town?"

"Yeah, me 'n Kate. She's looking to set up shop and I'm looking to defile my earth-bound flesh beyond recognition."

"Well, I don't think I can help you with your quest, but I'd sure love a game of cards." He grinned, knowing that Doc harboured a weakness for card sports that matched his own.

Doc obtained from his pocket a deck of cards. "You remembered. I'm touched."

Luke drained his beer. "It's how we met, if you recall."

Doc stretched the bottle across the table and splashed some whisky into Luke's empty mug. He took up the cards and began shuffling the deck. "How could I forget?" Doc leaned in closer and lowered his voice. "That was the night—what was his name?" he asked as he began to deal.

"Davis," Luke replied quietly. "Cramdon or some such—Davis."

"Ah, yes, the fool who was just as bad with a knife as he was with a hand of cards."

"Yes, well, too bad he didn't fall on his cards instead of his knife."

Doc doubled over, half coughing, half laughing. After expectorating, he turned back to Luke. "I'd forgotten how you make me laugh, son."

"You okay?" Luke asked.

"Sure, for a *dyin'* man." Luke made to inquire but Doc spoke before he could. "Come on, let's play poker and not talk of dismal matters."

Luke nodded and donned his best poker face. He tossed back some whisky and took up his cards. "I'm relieved you came in tonight, Doc. It's been hard digging up a decent game of poker with the desert creatures of the Dragoons." He glanced up to see Doc struggling to keep a straight face then muttered, "Damn prairie dogs mark their cards like it's their territory."

It was no good. Doc busted into a smile and chuckled. "You gonna play or be the floor show?"

"Both, I hope. It's so difficult to find an audience without yellow fever ticks."

"Shit," Doc murmured before laughing up more moisture.

After a few more sober hands, Luke asked quietly, "They still say I did it?"

"As far as I can tell, yes," Doc alleged while he rolled a cigarette. "Although I don't usually include myself in the company of bounty hunters and the like, I haven't heard anything to the contrary."

Luke nodded. The drunken Mr Davis had called Luke a cheat after losing a fair amount of money to him, and a fight had ensued. After falling against Luke during the mêlée, Davis had taken his own knife in the lung. Doc'd had a good view of the accident and created a diversion—a perfect mixture of hard alcohol and a smouldering cigarette butt. He'd then told Luke to lose himself—head West.

"I'm forever in your debt for saving my skin," Luke murmured sincerely.

Doc drew on his cigarette as it took to the flame of his lit match. After flicking the spent wooden sliver to the floor, he picked up the hand before him. "No need for all that. Just have enough to cover your losses tonight. I believe the paltry pot before us sports a staggerin' four whole dollars."

Luke smiled and laid down his hand face up. "Will this straight flush do?"

"Damn, boy. You are vicious at the table," Doc teased with a straight face and a gleam in his eye.

Chapter Seven

Allen had left Beatrice alone for days—longer than he had since he'd come to town. She'd taken the time to set in motion deliveries of everything she'd purchased. Most of the kitchen items were now stored on his cupboards ready for use. Very pleased with her choices, she sat smiling to herself as she stirred the nearly done stone soup.

She'd also remembered Allen's birthday was the following week and, as wife of the late minister, she felt it her duty to throw the man who'd brought life back to the church a surprise party. Perhaps this would give him other people in his life to pay attention to. In between the things she'd ordered for Allen, she'd also written and delivered invitations, arranged for food and a birthday cake for the celebration, and recruited the help of some of the older women in the flock of the Shepherd of the Hills to set things up the afternoon of the party. They'd promised her not only to decorate, but also to plan and execute a ruse to get Allen to the tent. If they accomplished what they'd set out to do, Allen's ego, like his brother's, would become flooded, swollen. He'd be obligated to broaden his friendship base with members of the community and leave her be.

"Mrs Gaitland," Ginny said, catching her breath, having just run up to Beatrice. "Ma had me doing all sorts o' chores 'round the house since after church this mornin', and time just got away from me."

"Don't you worry yourself over it—everyone's been served." Beatrice smiled. "I'm glad you came, though, I could use the company."

"Glad to help. Cookin's almost as fun as kissin'." Before Beatrice could gather her wits to comment on Ginny's outlandish remark, Ginny sat down on the bench next to her. "Smells good." She then changed the direction of the conversation faster than lightning. "Speakin' of kissin', where's Luke tonight?"

"For shame, Ginny—" But before she could continue to reprimand the girl, Beatrice's conscience choked out the rest of the admonishment. During the last few days, she had'nt had time to cast her gaze upon the handsome young man, but, as for her nights, well, her ardour had not cooled one little bit. "I don't know. I haven't seen him around lately." *In the flesh*, she added silently.

"That's because you've been busy," a masculine tone chimed in from behind Beatrice and Ginny.

Warm, breezy tendrils wound themselves around Beatrice's insides that had nothing to do with the season. She suppressed a smile and glanced over her shoulder at Luke. "Hello, sir," she said formally.

He chuckled and slapped his spoon against his thigh, stepping up to the cauldron next to Beatrice. "'Sir?' Does this mean I've gained the respect of my peers?"

Ginny leant back out of Luke's line of sight "He's got mine," she purred low, quite forward and far too informed when it came to matters of men and women.

Beatrice slid Ginny a cautionary look and cleared her throat. "Ready for some soup, Luke?" she asked, turning back to him.

"I'm ready for anything you have for me."

Ginny fairly swooned.

"Ginny." She interrupted her young friend's reaction before she made a spectacle of herself. "Would you please go and check the oil levels in the lamps inside the tent?"

"Oh, all right," Ginny grumbled. She stood and headed for the tent flap.

Beatrice took the bowl from Luke and spooned the thick beef stew into it. "And you'd better watch what you say, especially around others."

When he reached for his supper, Luke's manly hands cupped hers in a shrewd but brief gesture then slid away, the bowl secure in his grip. "Does this mean I get to say anything I like in private?"

"Not unless you are interested in losing a limb," she joked to ease the tension of their repartee, which was now dancing in a tempestuous whirl close to the edge of presumptuous.

Luke made no comment as the other miners came towards the cauldron in search of seconds.

"I'll take my chances," he murmured and passed dangerously close to Beatrice, upsetting her skirts, brushing up against the backs of her legs as he went.

"Ahem."

She turned to find Allen standing behind her a few feet away, trying to look aloof and unconcerned.

"I've always thought it a good sign in a pastor's wife that she be able to make friends with just about anyone," he said.

Startled at the sudden appearance of Allen, she turned her face away, unable to even begin to retrace the steps of her and Luke's conversation to try to figure out what her brother-in-law might have overheard. After a few moments she looked up. "Good evening, Allen." She smiled woodenly and continued ladling soup for the next man in line. "Soup?" she asked him without meeting his eyes.

"Uh, no, but thank you for the offer," he murmured patronisingly.

She nodded, keeping her concentration on not spilling a drop.

Out of the corner of her eye, she saw Allen glance over to where Luke had settled with his back against the nearest sturdy tree.

"I have some news," he said to her, but loud enough for everyone around the fire to hear.

"Do you?" she echoed, feebly attempting to sound interested.

"Yes. I've decided I'm going to get more involved with the community. I've been talking with Marshal White about the infestation of outlaws here in town, and I've asked how I can be of help."

"How very gallant of you," she murmured, glancing up at him but trying not to meet his direct gaze. For one thing, his self-importance was enough to make her eyes roll.

"Why, thank you." He sounded so self-satisfied she cringed inwardly. "Marshal White asked me to keep my ears and eyes open for any outlaws who might happen this way." He looked around at the miners and back to Beatrice. "He says a stack of brand-new wanted posters were delivered today, and I promised I'd study them at length. You know, peacekeeping has always intrigued me. I suppose one could call it sort of a hobby."

"Sounds fascinating," she replied, hiding a smile, pleased that her ruse seemed to be working.

Allen clasped his hands behind his back and he rocked back and forth from his toes to his heels. "I wouldn't doubt if I was to be deputised at some point."

"And just think, eventually you can run for mayor," she added, miraculously burying her sarcasm. She almost grinned when she heard Luke in the background choking on his laughter.

"Hmm." The noise came through Allen's nose as if he were considering it but was still unconvinced. "Well, I must be running along."

"Goodnight then," she uttered to Allen with an impassive slant of her head.

Allen walked away into the cover of night before he turned back to look at Beatrice. He observed her as she'd finished serving the last miner and was at that moment wiping her hands on her apron.

Allen drew his fists into his pockets as he watched the ragamuffin Luke approach her again. If she'd ignored him, it would not have been so irritating to Allen, but she was speaking animatedly to him and seemed far more engaged with him—in a most likely insignificant conversation—than she had been with Allen's announcement about helping the marshal. In fact, she'd sounded as if she didn't care if Allen lived or died.

"Damn them to hell," he muttered through gritted teeth, his jaw clenching as a new thought flitted through his mind. *What if Beatrice has given herself to the boy? It would be just like a widow to do something so unsavoury. Come to think of it, what was her allowance being spent on?* He knew. *She must be spending it on that little prick, Luke. It should be me sliding my dick between her legs, clearing out the cobwebs my brother likely left her with, not the self-confident pauper.* Allen's head was beginning to ache.

He folded his arms in disgust. Something drastic had to be done about their affair, and fast. But what? Too many things were buzzing around in his mind to think rationally. What he needed was a shot or two of spirits and a quick fuck to clear his head. He turned away from the quaint little scene and headed for his hotel room. He'd change his clothes and sneak out the back way. Finding a whore on the edge of town would be easy. Finding one who reminded him of Beatrice, even in the dark, would prove difficult.

* * * *

From a deep sleep, Beatrice heard shouting. The acrid smell of thick smoke permeated her lungs. Choking, she leapt out of bed, her heart pounding in fear for her life and, in the back of her mind, her few possessions. After sliding her feet into her boots and ignoring their ties, she broke into a run and made it out of the front door, nearly slamming into Allen.

"I can't believe you've come out undressed and naked for all the world to see," he snarled at her.

Can his sensibilities possibly be so delicate as to think a nightgown is the same as being naked? "In case you haven't noticed, Allen, my house is burning down!"

"It's only the back porch, Beatrice." Allen gave her one of those angry looks reminding her of her late husband and she simply snapped.

"Well, then. Shall I call for a maid to coif my hair as well?" she enquired in mock coyness, wadding her hair in her hands and holding it on the top of her head.

Huffing in exasperation so only she could hear, Allen removed his coat and placed it around her shoulders just in time for her to jump out of the way of the fire brigade.

As the line of water buckets began creeping their way in the direction of her darling cottage, Allen shooed her to safety. "Go on, my dear, take yourself safely away from here." He pointed down the hill, being sure to sound like the hero to everyone within hearing range.

By the light of the moon she found an out-of-the-way spot near some trees at the bottom of the hill where she could watch the gallant efforts of the townspeople.

In fear of losing everything, Beatrice gripped the edges of Allen's coat. Then she recalled his comment about the porch. How had he known? Tears formed and blurred her vision. It was all too much to take in as the thought occurred to her that perhaps this was Allen's way of bringing her officially under his wing. He'd start with the porch and weasel his way towards destroying what little she had left, including her dignity.

A voice enquired from behind her, pulling her from her musings. "Are you unhurt?"

Beatrice knew exactly who it was, and her heart jumped a bit at the warmth she heard. She blinked away her tears and felt the tightness in her shoulders ebb a bit, but didn't want to make a scene by reaching up to knead the muscles at her neck. Keeping her eyes forward she answered him. "I am well, thank you. Did you happen to see who did this?"

"I wish I knew, but I was asleep down near the creek. The shouts of the men woke me up—"

Suddenly remembering her unbound hair, she reached for it, Allen's coat falling to the ground, forgotten in her belated endeavour to be decorous. She pulled the long, wild waves over her shoulder, twisting them into a rope, readying it for a knot.

"Wait. Don't hide your hair," he commanded gently.

"But, Luke, it is unseemly for me to—"

"Please, Beatrice, let your hair go. I want to see it," he whispered, mere inches away from her ear.

"Luke—"

"Please." His voice seemed to ache with need. "I have nothing soft in my life. Let me have this one little pleasure."

Beatrice swallowed, looking up the hill at the people who were being directed by her brother-in-law to put out the fire. She was being silly. She hated to think of Luke sleeping on the hard ground, only bathing in the cold stream. Perhaps, when the fire was finished destroying her beloved cottage, her plight would be the same. At the single thought her tears rushed forward once again. With the barest of nods, Beatrice pushed the handful of hair over her shoulder and down her back.

Immediately, his hands were in her hair and she shivered, the sensation chasing away her fears. Her nipples, free from the constraints of her corset, puckered tightly under her nightgown, and goose bumps ran in waves over her skin from her scalp to her toes. His breath and touch in her hair almost made her knees buckle—it must have been the purest form of sin she'd ever experienced.

And it was so good.

A rumbling groan came from the man behind her— the one entwined in her hair, wrapping himself closer and closer to her heart. From the second he'd touched her, she'd surrendered to the sultry mist of his spell. If she wasn't careful, she'd be completely lost, along with her heart. Her nipples ached they were so hard now. She could almost say the same about the hidden nub of flesh between her legs, which seemed to be filling with an inexplicable pressure. If only her husband would have paid this kind of attention to her, perhaps she wouldn't be left longing for it now.

Beatrice managed to stifle a sob. The one person in town she could claim as family she simply detested and mistrusted beyond measure. The practical stranger at her back could have been holding a knife— could have been the one who set her house on fire. But somehow she knew down deep in her heart that Luke could be trusted.

"My God, you are so soft," he murmured.

Her breath caught as he pressed his lips to the hair at her neck. *He is kissing my hair*. She could have died right there and been happy. If she was doomed to seek kindness from an outsider, then so be it.

"That feels so wonderful," she whispered brokenly, without thinking.

Luke chuckled. "You mean all I have to do is pet you some and you'll melt for me?"

She turned her head slightly to speak to him. "I've never—That is to say, my husband—" Her voice trailed off, her cheeks burning like the fire at the top of the hill.

"Are you telling me he didn't touch you like this?"

Never had she spoken aloud of such intimate things with anyone. She shook her head.

"He was a bigger fool than I thought," Luke ground out, his emerging irritation evident. "What else didn't he do with you?"

She opened her mouth to reply, but could think of nothing to say.

"Well, your silence answers my question, doesn't it?"

She swallowed. "I beg your pardon?"

"Nothing. He did *nothing* with you. It's the reason why you all but burst into flames when we kiss."

His insolent presumptions—however true they were, caused her back to stiffen.

After a few cavernous moments had fallen between them, he asked quietly, "Had your marriage even been consummated?"

A short bark of nervous laughter escaped her lips. "Of course it had! What an awful thing to imply." She felt her ardour cooling at his insinuation. "In fact, we shouldn't even be discussing this. It's a private matter."

"I would be more than willing to show you what you've been missing out on," he offered in a sultry voice.

She imagined him grinning behind her and nearly groaned in ecstasy at his suggestion. She didn't trust herself with him, not after fantasising about him nearly every waking moment since he'd first spoken to her at Stone Soup Hour. Besides, who knew what else she would allow him if he continued to flirt with her in this manner?

"Oh, for heaven's sake, I can no longer be here with you." Beatrice pulled away from Luke and began walking back up the low hill.

"You mustn't forget your coat, Mrs Gaitland," he said in a teasing tone.

She couldn't possibly return to her brother-in-law without his coat. Balling her hands into fists and lifting her chin a notch, she turned on her heel and stormed towards Luke.

His breath hitched at the sight of her wild hair and the way it framed her from the top of her angelic face down to her gently flaring waist. She seemed to be moving in slow motion. Her white nightdress blew in the soft breeze, her strides causing the fabric to blow flush against her body. The skirt slipped between her legs, showing every curve of her thighs in the moonlight. It was, without a doubt, the most beautiful sight he had ever beheld.

He recalled how her soft clean hair had fallen over his hands and forearms, and his cock reared up once again at the thought. He'd buried his face in the silk strands and inhaled, detecting the citrus sent of lemon mixed with her own personal perfume. He imagined her bed linens smelling this good. God, how he longed to entrap himself with her in the luscious snare of her sheets.

She could be sweet as pie or decorous as any society matron — and here she was at this very moment, mad as a bobcat in the rain and utterly fetching to boot.

Someone needed to tell her she and Luke belonged together — and that *someone* was going to be him — right here, right now.

Beatrice reached for the coat but he held it in a firm grip. "There is an explicit chemical reaction between us, Mrs Gaitland."

She knew she'd have to pull her mourning excuse, it was her only defence—a rapidly weakening defence, but a solid one for now. "I am a widow, a recent widow," her strangled whisper hissed out from between her lips. "How many times do I have to explain it to you?" She tugged fruitlessly at the fabric of Allen's coat.

"And how many times must our bodies be consumed by the mere presence of each other before you admit your attraction?" He pulled on the object that suffered amidst their tug-of-war, forcing her to take another step closer to him.

She searched frantically for another justification. "I—I tolerate you only out of Christian charity!" She stumbled in her efforts to retrieve the garment.

Luke laughed harshly and let the coat drop. As quick as a striking snake, he took her by the waist and pulled her against his chest. Looking into her eyes he insisted, "You lie."

His low, deadly calm voice made her knees weaken, his strong hands about her waist nearly staggered her—the only thing that separated their skin was her thin cotton chemise. His touch seemed divine yet sinful. A chill swirled in her bosom beneath the white-hot branding of his hands. The obvious power he held was everything a man should possess—and right now she wanted nothing more than to be possessed by him.

But she couldn't possibly—

Chapter Eight

Luke grinned. "You're trembling." His gaze flickered from her eyes to her lips and back again. "You want me as much as I want you."

What could she do but cling feebly to her only alibi, which barely threatened to sway him? "There is the matter of my mourning period, sir." Against her will, the tears she'd been loath to shed were now making trails down her cheeks. "Were I to violate that institution, the congregation of Shepherd of the Hills —"

"We are both flesh and spirit — we can't possibly be just one or the other." Then, as if he had every right, he took her mouth in a searing kiss, but only for a moment or two. He pulled back just enough to blot away her tears with his lips. This touched her deeply. No one had ever done such to her in her lifetime.

He finished his task and smiled. "Yes, you do want me."

"Let me go," Beatrice cried brokenly as more tears filled her eyes, her self-control in shards on the ground at her feet. She shouldn't be here like this with him.

"Once you admit it and surrender, you won't feel so guilty," he said, as if he had read her mind. He drew a breath to continue when—to her surprise—he released her.

"And then what? There can be nothing done about what I think or what you feel." She shuddered and covered it by sniffing daintily. "I am in mourning and that is all there is." She gathered Allen's coat into her arms. Beatrice turned on her heel to go, only pausing briefly at his next words.

"Listen to me, Mrs Gaitland. You were married to the worst of men—a rat in a collar, who was and is unworthy of anyone's grief, however traditional."

The fire had been thoroughly doused by the time Beatrice reached the top of the hill.

"Dear, dear Beatrice," Allen said loud enough for all to hear. "Here you are. I was so worried—but the volunteers of this fine town have saved you and your home from ruin."

With tears in her eyes, which had nothing to do with the fire and everything to do with Luke, she thanked the volunteers of the fire brigade. Mercifully, only her back porch had been destroyed – the rest of her house remained intact.

Allen went on and on, playing the concerned hero. Beatrice let him. Perhaps the people would invite him to dine at their abodes, if only to alleviate her cooking schedule.

Later, as she lay her head down upon her pillow, she speculated as to the reason why she'd lost her porch in a fire. Was there a lesson to be learned here, or were there more sinister forces at work?

* * * *

While Beatrice prepared lunch in Allen's new kitchen, he announced he would, as of this very evening, assume full occupation of his house.

"Congratulations," Beatrice offered warmly, even though she dreaded him being so close. Allen's surprise party was at eight o'clock that night, but she'd needed a way to push the notion to the back of her mind so that the distraction wouldn't show in her eyes. Lindley had always possessed the ability to tell when her thoughts were elsewhere and it was likely his brother harboured the same talent. Determined not to draw Allen's attention, she concentrated on his settling in next door.

"Yes, well, someone needs to watch over you. You seem to get into trouble at every turn."

A warning shot fired from a cannon in the back of her mind, but she ignored it. She looked at him, slanting her head to the side. "If you are referring to the fire last night, I had nothing to do with it. Not a single one of my lamps were—"

Allen stepped forward and took her hand. "Now, now. I didn't mean to lay blame on anyone."

Beatrice relaxed just a bit and tried to pull away from his hold, nearly succeeding.

He frowned and held fast to her fingers. "Beatrice, do not shy away from my touch. We are family. More than family. I may be so bold as to—"

"No, Allen." She twisted from his grip. Facing the counter, she shook her head. "You are my late husband's brother—I'm thoroughly content to leave the situation as is."

"Well, I am not, Beatrice."

She had nothing to say to him. She'd hoped he would have understood by now that a sister-in-law, brother-in-law relationship was all she could tolerate between them. God, she could never be interested in him for any other purpose, particularly a physical one. The thought made her skin crawl.

A scant few heartbeats later he took an audible breath and spoke. "I am under the suspicion that your widow's yearnings have caused your thoughts to stray."

A block of ice settled in her stomach. She turned back to him, allowing the feeling of anger to blossom. "I'm not sure from what source you've garnered your information, sir, but, I assure you, my intentions to mourn the loss of my late husband are and always have been honourable, in every way." Disgusted with the familiar look of reproof on his face, she spun away from him and busied herself with placing a stack of clean plates in his cupboard.

"You know of whom I speak, Beatrice."

She refused to answer him.

"Yes, I think you do." Allen turned her to face him and wagged a finger in her face. "He's dangerous, Beatrice."

"Who is dangerous?" she asked, stepping out of his reach.

He narrowed his eyes at her. "You know perfectly well. That young vagrant, Luke. Has your allowance just slipped through your fingers or have you been spending it on him?"

"Oh, please." She rolled her gaze along the ceiling, refusing to spoil the surprise of his birthday party no matter what he accused her of. It sickened her to think that she had spent her time and money on a celebration for this mule of a man.

He continued to berate her, but her thoughts wandered. Beatrice was positive of Allen's ignorance as to the depths of danger Luke posed to her. Had she given in to her desires, not only would her reputation be lost, but her heart as well. Her position in society was important, but nothing could scar a woman's psyche like the breaking of a heart—and that sort of thing would stay with her no matter how far she ran from the situation. She was disinclined to live with either scenario, hence her adamant refusal of Luke's advances. He could have any woman he wanted. Once he was finished with her, he'd probably toss her aside for a woman more his age—or perhaps a woman not so used as she. Beatrice refocused on Allen, who had been moralising for the last ten minutes, with warnings and accusations.

"Think of it, why would someone with a strong back and quick mind choose to work as a lackey at a general store?" He continued when she didn't answer. "Because, Beatrice, he is running from something—most likely, the law."

"Allen, the boy is harmless. You are just saying this out of speculation."

"Be that as it may, if I find his face on a wanted poster, Beatrice, don't think I will hesitate for a moment in turning him in to the authorities."

She lifted her hands to stop his lecture. "I do not wish to discuss this further."

A knock sounded at the kitchen door.

"I'll answer—I'm expecting a delivery," he said, the last of his angry edge appearing to fade away as he readied himself to present a calm façade to the person at the door—just like his brother used to do.

As Beatrice seated herself at the table, Luke leaned in and set a crate of items in Allen's hands. A silent breath caught in her throat and she glanced at the open window next to the door. He must have heard her and Allen's conversation. It had, after all, been free of quiet discretion.

She watched Luke's face to see if she could detect if he'd been privy to their discussion, but the view of his eyes was obstructed from her sight. He had pulled his hat so far down on his head his ears must have been half covered.

Allen thanked him curtly. She noticed Allen hadn't tipped Luke, much to her irritation. Without sparing her a glance, Luke departed.

Beatrice took up her bread and spread butter on it, no longer hungry but going through the motions to appease the man who, in essence, was her judge, jury and executioner.

The food tasted like ash on her tongue.

It had been pure chance that Mr McElroy, who'd hired him more as a stock boy rather than a runner, asked Luke to do him the favour of delivering the crate to Allen's house this morning.

Luke had smiled with all sincerity at the store owner, of whom he was genuinely fond. It discomforted him no small amount that his employer hadn't the slightest notion that he'd been harbouring a fugitive from the law.

If his face did end up on one of those wanted posters he'd heard Allen talk about, he'd have to leave town, and that would mean leaving the company of his sweet young widow. No matter how sporadic their encounters were, he was loath to venture elsewhere.

At this very moment, Luke's pulse pounded in his ears as he made a beeline to his camp. He need to get out and quick. He had a sinking suspicion that his face *was* on one of those damn posters Allen had taken on the commission to study. Through the window Luke had heard that bastard proudly announce to Beatrice he would—

The memory of a brown-eyed girl bundled up in fancy Christmas furs flashed through Luke's mind, stopping him in his tracks.

"Peaches," he breathed in wonder and smiled. A riot of joy replaced the dread in his stomach.

* * * *

"Happy Birthday, Pastor Allen!" The thirty attendees inside the Shepherd of the Hills tent shouted, then burst into a rousing chorus of *For He's a Jolly Good Fellow* to an all but blushing Allen.

Smiling, Allen turned to face Beatrice. He snaked his arm around her waist, pulling her close in a possessive manner she quite found offensive.

She looked at him, glaring up into his eyes, her pleasant façade melted into a dark mask of fury. "Now you know where my allowance has been going," she said over the boisterous song, loud enough to only be heard by him. "You accused me of having an affair—this is the last surprise party you'll ever get from me, Allen Gaitland." She smiled, but her eyes still burned with anger. "I will now leave you to your adoring congregation." Sliding her thumb under his wrist, she peeled his arm from around her waist.

When the merrymakers finished singing Allen's praises and stepped forward to surround him, Beatrice faded into the background and slipped from the tent into the warm summer night.

Pausing a few yards away from the jovial gathering to wrap her arms around her middle, she gulped down a few breaths of air and looked into the sky, shedding the feeling of oppression she'd endured while standing next to Allen. The heaviness in the air testified to the humid evening, and a few clouds hung low overhead.

Involuntarily emulating the helpless rain clouds unable to shed their weighty moisture, neither would her tears fall. Tonight a good cry would have helped cleanse her weary soul. Her emotions had been bottled up for what seemed like weeks.

"Psst."

Beatrice raised her gaze, scanning the darkness of the moonless night in the direction from which the sound had come.

"It's me, Luke."

She spotted him between two cottonwoods. "What on earth —?"

"Why aren't you at *Pastor Allen's* party?"

A sarcastic puff of air escaped from between her lips and she lifted her gaze to the sky. "Perhaps it's because I'm sick of the sight of him."

He chuckled. "I don't blame you."

Stepping closer to him she asked, "What are you doing out here?"

Luke smiled in the darkness, his white teeth showing between his lips. "Waiting for you. I have wonderful news," he said in a soft voice.

This intrigued her to no end. "Do you?" she asked with a slight tilt of her head and took another step forward. And she didn't care what it looked like. She needed to feel his presence now more than ever.

He nodded once in confirmation. "But I can't tell you here."

"Why?"

"Never mind. Will you come with me?"

"To where?"

He looked around. "Away from here," he said, just above a whisper.

"Why can't you tell me now?"

He held out his hand to her. "Please?"

"Luke—"

"Come on, I want to go where we can talk."

"We are talking currently."

"No, we are whispering, afraid of being caught."

She made to protest further but couldn't. "Where are we going?"

"You'll see." He took her gently by the hand and guided her through the trees.

They walked in silence for some time, but her forbearance soon wore as thin as a ream of fifty-year-old organdie. Her nagging conscious prodded for at least a *hint* of what was on his mind and she finally gave in.

"What is all this about?"

"You will see."

"Have you struck it rich?"

"No."

"Are you getting married?"

He laughed. "No!" He slowed down a bit so she could walk by his side.

"Well, then, what is it?"

"Be patient. You will find out soon enough."

She chuckled. "If there is one thing I don't possess, it's the capacity for patience."

"It's not too much further."

`Not too much further' turned into another half-mile and Beatrice was ready to end the torture by digging her heels into the ground, demanding he return her to her cottage. On the verge of performing what she had in mind to do, they came to a clearing.

Luke escorted her over to a fallen log. A thick blanket covered the rough bark. "Please do sit down. Are you cold? Would you like me to light a fire?"

She shook her head as she sat, her eyes well used to the dark. "No, I'm fine. What is all this about?" she asked and surveyed her surroundings. He had obviously brought her to where he'd been sleeping. A bedroll and knapsack lay upon the ground next to a cold fire ring.

He paced before her, not quite knowing how to begin.

"Luke, what is it?"

He opened his mouth and shut it again.

"What?" she nearly shouted.

From his pocket he drew out a deck of cards.

She looked down at the cards then back up to him. "You brought me all the way out here to play cards?"

Luke grinned and began shuffling midair. "There once was a charming Christmas party—"

"It's August, Luke," she reminded him, speaking as if to a child.

He nodded. "We were visiting my cousin's family in Rhode Island—"

She sobered and sat up a bit straighter at the mention of her home state.

"We'd come all the way up from Virginia."

She didn't speak, her gaze falling briefly to watch his hands.

Luke smiled. "And what do you have to ante, Peaches?"

Chapter Nine

Beatrice inhaled and covered her mouth. A muffled "Oh my Lord" escaped from behind her fingers.

Luke's grin became a full-blown smile. "'Don't call me Peaches,' my cousin's beautiful best friend demanded in haughty tones. Her eyes were shooting daggers at me, the boy who had won trinkets and all sorts of other things from the children at the party. 'I'll tell you what,' I said to her, 'I'll bet, if I beat you at cards, I win the right to call you Peaches'. 'No,' she said adamantly. 'Why, afraid I might win?' She lifted her chin in a brave gesture and ordered me to deal."

She removed her hand from her mouth. "Lucas Hughson," she said in awe.

"I knew you looked familiar to me, Peaches. It's been bothering me for *days*."

She laughed. "It's been almost ten years since that card game. You don't have to call me Peaches anymore."

"Ah, but I won the right, remember?"

She shook her head, still unable to comprehend that someone from her past—someone who'd known her before she married and had been dragged off to this godforsaken desert—stood boldly before her. "How in the world did you come up with that nickname in the first place?"

Luke retired the cards to his pocket and folded his arms across his chest. He took a half-step towards her and spoke quietly. "When my cousin Alison first introduced you, I thought I heard her say your name was Peaches. 'Peaches Victoria King' she'd said. I knew it to be a strange name, but your glowing skin and apple-round cheeks told me it was the perfect designation."

"You called me Peaches for the rest of the day. I hated it." She smiled wryly.

"I know you did. But I also knew you would remember me long after I left your company." He unfolded his arms and reached out, his fingertips grazing her cheek with a featherlight touch.

"I did think of you after you left, you brat," she teased, then looked at him in awe. "How you have changed," she said, a scant puff of air away from breathless as she sought out the twelve-year-old boy in the face of the man before her.

Luke shrugged a shoulder and angled his head in a bashful manner.

"You are so fine, Luke," she whispered. "Had I known..." Her voice tapered off. She'd almost told him she would have waited for him.

Luke smiled, but his eyes implied that he'd read her thoughts.

She came to her feet. "I'm sorry, things—"

Luke took her face in his hands. "Shh, don't, Peaches," he said, shaking his head slowly and stroking her cheeks with his thumbs.

Her heart constricted. *If only things would have been different.* The thought brought some sense back to her. "I—I must, of course, insist you cease calling me Peaches."

"Do I need to beat you at another hand of cards?" he asked with a straight face.

A laugh disguised as a wheeze of air erupted from her, but died quickly as he was pulling her closer to his face. "Luke, I can't."

"You still feel the same about your mourning then?" he asked, a hair's-breadth away and staring at her lips.

She couldn't speak, couldn't even move.

Luke drew air into his lungs and released her. "I'll tell you what. I'll only call you Peaches when we're alone." He sat down on the log as if astride a horse.

"Luke, I told you, we can't be alone." Settling herself before him on the log, she looked into his eyes.

"We are alone now, sweetheart," he murmured. His hands rose as if he were going to pull her into another embrace. She stiffened and his hands fell to his thighs. "You mustn't fight your heart."

At that instant, she felt he was going to spring to his feet. Unable to bear the thought of him doing so, she quickly changed the subject.

"What did you do with your life after that Christmas party?"

He was touched over her concern, which set him more at ease. "Well, when I became of age, I attended Columbia University."

"My father's alma mater. Did you enjoy it?"

Luke shrugged. "I liked playing football."

Beatrice grinned and he caught her gaze as it rolled over him, as if cataloguing his physique. He was sure she had no idea how dangerously flirtatious it was to do such to a man who wanted with all his heart to make love to her. The thought occurred to tell her so, but he enjoyed it far too much to mention it and possibly stop future assessments. Instead, he continued. "Afterwards, I decided I wanted to take the easy road, wanted to do something which required no thought at all. So I announced to my family that I didn't want to take over the plantation, and I wanted to become a professional gambler."

For the merest of moments, her jaw dropped open and she gasped. "I know you are good at playing cards, but your declaration must have horrified them."

"Like you wouldn't believe." He shook his head. "My father couldn't even invoke a civil phrase to utter to me until the morning I left for Atlantic City."

"So then what did you do?"

"I set out to make my fortune. I did very well at the tables, but the violence got worse the further west I travelled." He glanced away for a moment, hoping to find the right words. "I got in pretty deep."

"Oh."

Luke changed the subject to try to ease her mind. "I haven't asked you how you came to be here in Tombstone, because I already know."

"Really, how?"

He gave her a wink. "It's easier than winning at cards with a blind man to get the women of this town to sit down for a gossip session."

She laughed, a sound he preferred to any other in the world. "No matter how many times Lindley preached on the evils of gossip, it did nothing in the way of stopping the daily deluge."

"In defence of said harpies," he teased, "they only told me you were the widow of the late minister of Shepherd of the Hills Church—this was before I'd introduced myself to you. It pretty much explained to me why you were here."

She glanced down at her folded hands resting in her lap. Her bashful side made Luke long to hold her in his arms and let her know that her world could be so much happier if she'd just let him in.

After a moment or two of companionable silence, she raised her head and spoke. "So, how did you come to be in Tombstone?"

Luke inhaled and looked up into the stars. "I got into a scuffle at a table and a man was killed. My friend, Doc Holliday, whom I'd played with several times before the incident, saw the exchange. After acknowledging privately that the man's death wasn't my fault, he told me I'd better get out of town. So I left—headed out this way."

"But why didn't you stay and declare your innocence?"

He returned his gaze to Beatrice. "Because the deceased Mr Davis' brother was the town sheriff."

"Ah, I see." She paused, the wheels in her pretty head clearly spinning so that it shone in her eyes. Her barefaced intelligence was one of the things he loved about her. "Do you think, if we could locate the man who knows you are innocent, he would defend you?"

Luke removed his hat and tossed it towards his bedroll. "That's where it gets complicated." He sighed and drew his fingers through his hair.

"How so?"

"Well, Doc has been involved in a few incidents himself which have not reflected well on his character—as far as the law is concerned, that is."

She shook her head. "But the past shouldn't matter. A man's word is a man's word."

Beatrice's confidence in his situation made him want to pull her to him all the more. When he hesitated, she leaned into him. Her warm body felt wonderful—like a shelter in a storm. She sagged against his chest and he inhaled, taking in her feminine scent.

"I know," he murmured and kneaded the backs of her shoulders, "but it doesn't always work that way."

She buried her face against his neck. "But you are innocent."

Luke gave her a squeeze. To have his Peaches agree with him and show her support in such a way was heaven itself. A lump of heart-wrenching emotion formed in his throat at her declaration.

Suddenly, she felt homesick, worse than she had since Lindley dragged her across the country from town to town, all those years ago. She missed the balmy New England nights, the blatant change of seasons and the turn of the leaves in autumn. She missed her mother and sisters. But, most of all, she missed feeling safe. Appalled at herself but unable to stop the tide, she began to cry.

Luke swallowed audibly and began to rock her like a child in his arms. "What is it, love?"

It took a few moments for her to trust her voice. "This is all wrong, all of it. You should be a wealthy man, in a fine house surrounded by your friends." She took a breath that turned into one sob, then another. "I shouldn't be here either." She sniffed. "My mother was right, you know. She told me Lindley wasn't the man for me, and that marrying him would be a terrible mistake. God, how my proper British mother would love to hear those words now from her 'modern, Americanised daughter'."

"It seems we've both made our beds," he commented tenderly. "You and I had beautiful homes which we wandered away from like regular prodigals."

She nodded. "Lindley used to tell me my home life was evil, and that it was easier for a camel to slip through the eye of a needle than for a rich man to enter the kingdom of Heaven."

Luke gave her another squeeze. "It sounds like he was preparing you to live like a pauper."

"You're right." She sniffed. "That's exactly what he was doing."

"Well, just so you know, it's nonsense for you to feel guilty about living high—America was founded on the concept of being able to make a living however you want—make as much money as you want. And if the lazy people don't like it they can leave on the first boat across the ocean."

She smiled, tilted her head and looked up at him. "You know, you are the first person I've run into in years who's made any sense."

Luke glanced down at her then back up to the sky. "Yeah, well, all you've had to talk to is a mangy scarecrow and a few tumbleweeds."

Sobbing and laughing at the same time, she nodded in agreement.

For the longest while, they talked of home, the green lawns, the garden parties, the brandy and cigars after supper for the men and tea for the ladies, seasons of cotillions and balls.

"I could picture you in a fine, burgundy taffeta gown, sweeping into a ballroom and knocking all the men off their feet."

She giggled. "I see you dressed in all black for supper, a cigar in one hand and a ragged deck of cards in the other, like the one you have in your pocket right now."

Luke chuckled. "This is the deck I won the other night from Doc — and, I can tell you, he was less than pleased to part company with it."

"He isn't angry, is he?"

"No, no. In fact, I'll probably let him win it back from me one of these nights," Luke said with the casual elegance of a man confident in his abilities.

Relaxing once again in his arms, Beatrice sighed.

"Sadly, I fear it was the arrival of Doc which spawned the interest in the wanted posters by the law. I suppose they are looking to see if they can't cash in on Holliday."

"How awful," Beatrice declared. "I'll look at the wanted posters Allen has to see if your friend is named on one of them. And, if I find one with you on it, I'll burn it."

"I cherish your enthusiasm, Peaches. However, other towns have their own set of posters."

After a few heartbeats, she asked, "What will happen if there is a poster of you and they catch you out here, all alone with no one to defend you?"

Luke shrugged. "I'll probably be hanged."

She clung to him. "Never! I won't let it happen!"

"Sweetheart —" He shook his head for emphasis. "I'm afraid you'll have no say in the matter."

"I know — What if we went away from here and returned home, in a united front? Surely our families would forgive us?"

"I'd be glad to, but only if I am free to do so. Hell, they may have a couple of Pinkerton's watching my ancestral home as we speak. If I'm arrested, the location of the town being immaterial, there won't be much either of us can do." He nuzzled her cheek with his. "A man lost his life and I am the prime suspect. The way to absolution for some is to lay blame."

"But, Luke, I've just found a bit of home and I can't lose it now." She pulled away just enough to look into his eyes. "I can't lose *you* now."

An eternity stretched between them before she spoke again. "What I said — the night of the fire — "

"I know. You don't need to apologise."

"Yes, I do. I didn't mean — "

"You were just speaking out of anger."

She knew he was trying to save her from the embarrassment of confessing her thoughts, but she had to continue. Needed to. "Speaking out of desperation, more like."

Luke searched her eyes as if looking for an explanation.

She turned away. "You've been right all along. I am attracted to you. I think about you, I dream of you — it's nearly unbearable." She ended in a whisper. When he didn't respond, she looked to his face for a sign of some sort, an emotion — telling her she hadn't exposed her heart for nothing.

Luke's gaze dropped to Beatrice's lips.

She wanted him to kiss her, damn it all! She'd wanted it for so long it seemed there had been nothing in her life before this moment. Hang the rules of mourning — and hang Allen for that matter!

She focused on his mouth. "I'll do whatever it takes to help you out of this awful misunderstanding. You are the bravest man I've ever met, Lucas Hughson."

She couldn't be sure, but it felt as if she'd met Luke halfway for the kiss. And she was pleased to her toes that it had happened so, because he really knew how to kiss a woman. His lips tickled and teased, his tongue soothed and bewildered her. He smelt of smoky wood, but fresh like the outdoors. He pulled her to him with his strong arms and her heart hammered in her chest. Each time he'd kissed her it had left an indelible mark on her soul, but this—

Suddenly, he scooped her up and carried her over to his bedroll—and, by God, she didn't care what happened from here. If Allen was already convinced she'd been having an affair and had punished her for it, then she would allow herself to commit the sin.

Luke stopped kissing her and caressed her face with his heated gaze. He looked as if he wanted to say something, but she spoke first.

"Go ahead, I'm ready." She squeezed her eyes shut.

"What?" he asked, sounding terribly confused.

"You may lift my skirts now."

"And do what?"

Her eyes fluttered open to look at him. "Why, take me, of course."

"Holy—is that how your husband made love to you?"

She found herself gnawing on her bottom lip in embarrassment and nodded.

Luke helped her to her feet and spun her around so that her back pressed to his chest. "Now," he said, a tremor of raw emotion in his voice, "I want you to forget everything you know about what a man and a woman do together in bed, do you understand?"

She nodded and felt the side of her dress being unlaced, and quite deftly so.

"If you think God intended for a man to just lift the skirts of his wife and poke at her incessantly, you have no real grasp of the Almighty."

"Incessantly? No. Two or three pokes was usually all it took."

She heard Luke nearly choke behind her. "I think your late husband has taken the prize for the worst lover in the history of the world."

After a few swishes of fabric over her head, the entirety of her underpinnings fell in a pile near her feet. She stood with her back to him, totally naked. Luckily, the stars didn't afford much light. She shivered, but not because of the night air.

Suddenly his hands were in her hair, pulling pins and tossing them to the ground. When her hair was loose and hanging about her hips, he pressed himself against her back. He inhaled at her neck the way he'd done the night of the fire, and those same delicious goosebumps skittered up her arms and over her chest.

"God made woman from the rib of Adam," he murmured. "Eve had just as many fascinating spots on her body as Adam did." He massaged her neck in luscious circles. "It is my firm belief that God challenged Adam to find each and every one of those spots, any way he could. And take his time doing it."

Good Lord! He intends to find my spots! She swallowed and lifted her hands to cover her naked front.

In a flash, Luke took hold of her forearms. "There is no need to hide."

"But—but I'm fully unclothed."

"Yes." She could hear the smile in his voice. "Just like Eve."

Dropping her defences and any further thoughts of concealment, she sank back against him, trusting him with her body, her life.

He swept the ends of her hair away from her hips and let his hands follow her curves. "So soft," he exhaled the words. Everywhere his fingers grazed her skin, delicious shivers followed. She became aware of her own inhalations — they were more like gasps, small and fluttery like the wings of a butterfly.

He caressed her hips from back to front, then his hands began a slow ascent up her ribs. Thinking she may expire at the whisper-softness of his touch she rested her head back onto his sturdy shoulder and stared, unseeing, into the night sky. She thought her legs would not be able to support her if he continued his sensual appraisal of her body.

When he fondled her breasts she moaned his name. He kneaded her flesh, catching the tips between his fingers, tugging gently and releasing them again. The feeling was exquisite, his skill in the ways of love evident. Beatrice trembled from the inside out, willing the world to stop turning for them.

She felt his touch travel down her belly to the triangle of hair between her legs, but when he parted her, revealing her moist folds to the elements, her knees buckled.

Luke caught her by the waist. "Easy, there is still more I want to show you," his voice rumbled in her ear.

Beatrice found herself seated against his thighs as he leaned on the fallen log, his legs between hers. He tickled a trail back down between her thighs and she could have swooned. She looked down and observed his hands on her body, shocked at what she was watching him do, but unable to look away.

"You feel so good," he commented softly, next to her ear.

Mercy, he must have been watching, too. She nodded once, unable to vocalise an opinion. She nearly sighed aloud when his slick fingers slid lower to her opening. He didn't enter, but circled her, agonisingly slowly, teasing her wet skin. Then, when his other hand delved into her folds to find her rigid bit of flesh, she cried out something unintelligible.

Trapped between his arms and held there by his hands, Beatrice felt one of those episodes building behind where his fingers so skilfully excited her.

Her breathing became shallow as Luke lightly strummed his fingers over her in a wicked rhythm that drove her closer and closer to the edge.

Luke began breathing words into her ear, words she wouldn't have understood before, and even now was incapable of finding their definitions, but, oh, how she could feel what they meant.

"You are there, love, nearing that delicious threshold. I can feel you getting wetter the more I play with you."

At his words she held her breath as the wave built inside her. She floated above it awaiting the crash, anticipation making her tense.

"Yes, that's it. Feel my touch take you over the knife's edge."

God, how she yelled when she found her release.

His fingers, which that had been circling her opening, sank inside, sending more of her rapturous moans echoing beyond the campsite. Her insides clenched at his intrusion, and squeezed in a thrilling, fast-paced flicker.

Her muscles gave one last jerk as he removed his fingers from her body, only to graze her nub for a final tease.

"I want you, Peaches," Luke murmured. "Let me teach you…show you…fill you."

"Yes," was the only word she could produce—the only answer she wanted to give him.

Luke helped her back to his bedroll and, in mere seconds, he was free of his clothes and hovering between her legs she had spread for him in welcome.

"I've waited so long for this," he uttered the soft words with reverence and awe.

"Hurry," Beatrice whispered. "Please — I want to feel you."

He pushed into her, her slick folds accommodating him as if she were fashioned for him. She could feel every inch as he sank to the hilt. She moaned as the echo of tremors from his earlier attentions quivered in her now-full channel. "Luke," she panted. "You're like heaven inside me."

Luke groaned and began moving, his hips nuzzling hers. "You are so, so sweet and your heat — my God."

She watched him, nearly breathless with the sensations he was stirring within her. He held himself above her, the muscles in his arms bulging as he strained against her. Lord, but he was beautiful. She reached up and smoothed her hands over his shoulders and on to his chest. "This power you hold in check — and yet you treat me like a fragile china cup."

He paused, an inquisitive look passing over his features. "You want it a bit rougher, do you?"

With her cheeks burning at full blaze, Beatrice drew her bottom lip between her teeth. *How does one answer such a question?* She brought her shoulder up in a slight shrug and her head tipped towards it. Then, as if she'd found courage for the first time in her life, she nodded.

"That's my girl." Luke reached down and bent one of her knees. He scooped a hand beneath it and hooked it over his shoulder. He went much deeper than before, her sheath wrapped around him, producing an exhilarating compression. With her courage rising to unprecedented heights, she bore down on him, squeezing with all her might.

"Christ," he groaned. "I'll never get enough of your tight pussy."

With that he drove into her, pushing deep inside over and over again—just the way she'd asked him to. Beatrice's soul soared as violent waves of pleasure rocked her body, her voice a chorus of approval.

With wide eyes and her lungs fighting to catch up with the frantic beat of her heart, she looked up at her lover. He was smiling, still moving within her.

"You came fast, my little wanton. And I've barely begun to make love to you." With that, he began anew—pounding into her, releasing the tempest yet again.

* * * *

Luke had taken her in at least three more positions before he sat her down on his lap, facing him, her slick heat surrounding his satisfied cock.

"That was the best one," Beatrice said shyly as she clung to his shoulders, her breathing nearing normal.

He smiled. "You said that already."

"Did I?"

"Mmm-hmm." He nodded. "Four times now."

"Oh." She giggled.

Luke put his arms around her, pulling her close. "I should probably be getting you home soon." In opposition of his declaration, he didn't move a muscle.

She sighed, without reply.

He knew she didn't want to go, and he was in total agreement, but was loath to do any more damage than he'd possibly done to her reputation.

"Luke?"

"Hmm?"

"Thank you."

He hugged her tight in response.

"I never imagined it could be so wonderful."

"Now you know."

He felt her nod, her silky hair rasping against his ear and cheek.

A rooster crowed somewhere in the distance, alerting Luke and Beatrice to the fact that the sun would be encroaching upon the land within hours.

"Come on, our time here is at an end."

He helped her to stand then ushered her over to where their garments lay, strewn about the ground.

Chapter Ten

Luke and Beatrice reached the edge of her property. The wispy clouds had moved on and a few stars still twinkled in the sky — although they were beginning to wink out one by one. The breeze began to pick up as it normally did this time of morning, disturbing the leaves on the trees above and stirring her normally bound hair.

Luke pulled her close under the cottonwood trees at the bottom of the hill near her cottage. He wrapped her in his arms. She sighed.

"I am so glad I dragged you out into the wilds tonight." He nuzzled her cheek.

"So am I," she whispered. "You will take care of yourself, won't you, Luke? You won't let anything..." She tapered off, not wishing to finish her query.

Luke skimmed his hands over her shoulders and down her arms. "I promise I'll stay out of harm's way."

He pulled back and took her face in his hands. He kissed her goodbye, his lips passing softly over hers, tickling her. Lord, even after an entire night of love, she still wanted more, wanted him.

When he released her, she reached into his pocket, took out the deck of cards and held it between her palms. "Insurance to facilitate your returning to me." She grinned.

Luke smiled. "Trust me, you don't have to worry about that, Peaches." He kissed her once more then he was gone.

She trudged up the hill and entered her cottage, her entire body stiff from exercise and humming with the echoes of ecstasy.

Changing into her nightdress, she then climbed into bed, all the while reliving in her mind the intimate moments with Luke. She drifted off to sleep, sated like never before.

* * * *

"Beatrice?" Allen's voice accompanied his pounding upon her door. "Are you all right?"

Still engulfed in a drowsy bliss, Beatrice heard his voice and stretched beneath her sheets, not in any hurry to answer the irritating call of her brother-in-law as he jangled the knob of the front door, rattling the new deadbolts she'd had installed. She sat up. It must have been straight up noon.

Beatrice donned her wrapper and shuffled into the parlour, feeling smug about the stiff muscles in her legs—a secret she'd keep tucked away in her heart, safe from the intrusive Allen. She unbolted the door and opened it a crack to view with one eye the annoyance on her front porch. "Yes?"

Allen placed his hand on the door and applied pressure. "Are you all right? You didn't answer last night and have been in bed all day long," he whined and shifted his weight forward.

She held fast to the door. "I must have the flu, Allen. I'm all sore and still very sleepy."

Allen let the door go and took a half-step back. "Oh, well, that explains your sour behaviour last night."

Sorely tempted to slam the door in his face, she gripped the handle hard. "If there is nothing else —" She made to shut him out but he stopped her.

"Beatrice, have you finished the curtains for my study, yet? The light is so bright it gives me a headache."

Lord, could he be a baby when he wanted something. "I'll have them for you in a couple of hours or so."

He brightened. "Oh, good. Can you also go to the general store and see if the rest of my things have arrived?" he asked, clearly ignoring her illness, alleged or not.

She grinned, thinking she may run into Luke. "I will."

He returned her smile and left the porch.

Realising Allen must have thought she was smiling at him, she shrugged. *Who cares what he thinks?*

* * * *

It was Mr McElroy himself who had assisted Beatrice with Allen's order earlier that morning. When she'd asked him where his helper was, he'd told her Luke had come in and quit.

"The boy entered, thanked me, and said he had to be moving on. I paid him for the last few days he'd worked for me, o' course." Mr McElroy shook his head. "You were right, Mrs Gaitland, he was a good worker. I'm sorry I lost him."

In contrast to her pleasant smile, her blood ran cold. *What happened to facilitate his need to leave? It certainly wasn't our interlude last night.* She averted her gaze, unable to think about Luke right now. She had to get into Allen's study and find those wanted posters.

She dropped off a fresh loaf of bread and some berry preserves at her place, then she and Mr McElroy continued to Allen's house. After Allen's delivery was set upon the counter, Mr McElroy bade them farewell and hurried back to his shop.

Beatrice now sat in Allen's study, thinking of her earlier conversation with Mr McElroy while she hemmed the last brown and ivory brocade curtain panel. Allen pored over the papers on his desktop and rearranged them as he mumbled about this nose or that moustache, obviously going over the wanted posters.

"So," Allen said in a reserved voice, as if deep in thought but keeping up cordiality, "where was your young friend Luke this morning?"

Had Allen looked at her when he'd enquired about her lover, her calm façade would have crumbled. Stabbing the needle into the fabric for the last few stitches, she answered simply, "I have no idea."

"Hmm."

After a few moments, she found the courage to look up at him. "You seem very occupied today."

"Yes, well, we are narrowing in on one or two of these criminals." He indicated his desktop and the stack of papers.

Her heart leapt. "Really? Who?" She should not have allowed the words to fly out of her mouth in such a manner, but they escaped before she could stop them.

"Oh" — he waved a hand in dismissal — "this is men's work. You wouldn't be interested."

"Allen, I live in this community, too." Tying off the last stitch, she gritted her teeth behind her pleasant façade.

"My dear, leave the safety to the strong, more capable citizens and just go on about your business."

She stood and turned her back to him, the anger causing heat to burn a path up her neck to her face. How dare he tell her to mind her own business? Shaking off her annoyance, she focused on her objective — to get a look at those posters.

She went about the room slipping the curtains onto rods above each window, waiting for Allen to leave his study. Frustrated and impatient, she had to do something. "Allen, I'd sure like a cup of tea," she hinted, hoping to have a few moments alone with the items on his desk.

"So would I, thank you," he replied.

Growling under her breath, she made to exit Allen's study. As she passed the desk, she slowed, her eyes taking in the faces laid out on his desk as quickly as possible.

Obviously sensing her perusal, Allen gathered the papers into a stack and sat back in his chair, practically hugging them to his chest.

She shot an irritated look at the side of his head and headed for the kitchen to boil water for the tea that she hadn't really wanted in the first place.

Matching Beatrice's temper, the water was nearly at a boil when she heard a knock at the front door. Holding her breath, she waited for Allen to answer it. This was her big chance to go through those cursed posters.

"Beatrice, would you be a dear and see who is at the door?"

Rolling her hand into a fist, she almost pounded the wooden counter. Instead, she answered the door. It was the post.

On a small tray, she brought Allen his tea and the missive the postman had delivered. When she set the tray down, he was still huddled over his hoard of papers and she couldn't get even a glimpse of a single one.

As she went about the room gathering her sewing items and placing them in her basket, she heard Allen oohing and awing over the contents of the letter.

"I will be heading back to the cottage now, Allen," she announced, not wanting to spend another moment in his company.

"Very well," he responded, still focused on the message. "Oh, they found him, did they?" he murmured.

"Who?"

Allen glanced up at her, grinning patronisingly. "Never mind, young lady."

She exhaled, trying to convey her dissatisfaction. "Allen, I'm going to ask you a question and I want a straightforward, no-nonsense answer."

He gave her his full attention, resting his wrist on the desk before him, his fingers still gripping the letter. He raised his eyebrows as if in expectancy.

"What does the letter in your hands say?"

A moment passed and he relaxed. "It merely states that some lawmen have gone after a man this morning, an outlaw they have been tracking for some time now, and I am invited to supper this evening to discuss the success."

Her heart pounded loudly, as if it were wedged between her ears. "Who?"

"Who what, dear?"

"Whom did they go after?" she demanded.

Allen looked down at the missive. He scanned it from top to bottom then looked up at her. "How about that? It doesn't say." His lips curled into a satisfied, closed-mouth smile.

* * * *

Beatrice stormed through her door and into her kitchen. She tossed her sewing basket on the counter, nearly upsetting the jar of preserves she'd dropped off earlier.

"Lord, what an arrogant so-and-so he is!" She choked on the near curse she'd uttered. She paced her floor and suffered her nails digging into her palms. "Who does he think he is?"

Her heart gave a squeeze. "Luke," she whispered. He'd quit Mr McElroy's today, and all Allen's smug talk about catching an outlaw...

She needed to find Luke, and fast. Her stomach flipped over at the thought of him being caught and her lungs constricted, making it difficult to draw in air. Dumping the contents of her sewing basket onto the counter, she stuffed into it any kind of food she could get her hands on.

Beatrice paused. Would she be able to retrace her steps to Luke's camp? Her only hope in finding it was if she left from the Shepherd of the Hills tent, for that was the route they'd originally taken. She wasn't of the disposition to have paid any attention to the path when he'd walked her back home this morning. She'd have to make sure she was not followed, not by anyone, even if she had to double and triple back.

With panic hard on her heels, she hastily left for Shepherd of the Hills, clutching her basket of food.

* * * *

Beatrice circled the empty clearing, her heart in her throat. No evidence could be found of Luke, or ought of his gear. In this clearing they'd made love all night long—in this clearing she'd found her own personal paradise and had finally, *finally* discovered what it felt like to be a woman. She set her basket on the fallen log they'd leaned against last night when he'd shown her what her body was capable of, what they were capable of together. She looked over to where his bedroll had been and recalled the ecstasy he'd given her, her emotions a tug-of-war between melancholy and fear.

She glanced around the camp one more time. Utter hysteria bubbled up from her stomach and threatened to cause her to vomit when a familiar masculine voice addressed her from nearby.

"I am the luckiest man in the world if my Peaches happens to have food in her wee basket."

She swung around and launched herself into Luke's arms. Her tears poured forth, accompanied by great sobs of happiness. "I thought they'd taken you. Oh, Luke, I would've died had they done so." She clung to him, not caring if her arms felt as if they would break from hugging him so tightly.

Luke soothed her, cooing soft words to her regarding his safety. "It's all right, sweetheart. They haven't found me."

She pulled away as a dozen fragmentary questions tumbled from her lips. "Mr McElroy—your things—I couldn't find you—"

"Shhh." He wiped away her tears with his knuckles and placed a finger over her lips. "We'll have time to talk in a little while, but for now we need to get out of here."

She let him go but did not move away. "Where are we going?"

Luke grinned down at her. "How about a tropical island somewhere?"

Having come nearer to hysteria than she'd ever been before, she gasped, half laughing, half crying. "I would love that." She pressed herself to his chest. "Just the two of us," she murmured, her voice muffled by his coat. It smelt so much like Luke that climbing inside with him crossed her mind.

Kissing the top of her head, Luke turned her towards the brush and scooped up the basket. They headed up into the Dragoon Mountains, winding their way around more than a few intimidating craggy boulders.

They came to a dirt cave. "Here it is, home sweet home. Well, for now, anyway."

The old cave was a shallow twenty-feet deep, with the evidence of a recent cave-in making up the three angled walls. A few pieces of timber were wedged up near the ceiling, which may have held the original integrity of the dirt tunnel. It had clearly been an entrance to a mine. "Is it safe?" she asked, focusing on the deluge of fresh dirt with no small amount of trepidation.

Luke shrugged. "More or less. I wouldn't go shooting off a cannon or anything—"

With a chuckle, she felt her shoulders relax and she entered.

She came to rest on his bedroll and opened her basket. They ate while Luke told her what happened earlier that morning.

"I waited until sunrise, and was on my way to Mr McElroy's store when I passed by a window sporting one of those wanted posters with my face on it. It wasn't a very good likeness, but I figured I'd better get while the gettin' was good." He handed her another piece of bread spread with preserves.

"I'm glad you did. However, I was distraught with worry. I had tried to see the posters in Allen's study, but he wouldn't allow it." She took a bite of bread.

"It's all right now, Peaches. You don't need to put yourself in his company unnecessarily ever again."

She smiled and leaned her elbow on the basket handle, relieved to be there with Luke and thankful beyond words for his support. Experiencing a significant improvement in her mood, she cocked her head to the side and decided to tease him just a bit. "You jealous?" she asked with her mouth full.

"Hell yes, I'm jealous. He acts as if you're his private maid at his beck and call, while I'm hiding out here, unsure if I will be jeopardising us both if I try to see you."

She swallowed. She wasn't sure how far she could go with him, but she was willing to tempt the dangerous line of his tolerance. "Hm. I think I like it when you act covetous."

After a few anticipatory moments lagged by, she thought she saw something wicked flash across his face. Luke narrowed his eyes at her in a very predatory way that set her heart to pounding. He placed his bread in the basket, his fine lips curling into a sensual snarl.

If she didn't know him, her instincts would have told her to run. Perhaps she should run. A chase would only add to the thrill building in her breast. At the last possible second, she decided she'd better stay where she was. He began to crawl towards her like some wild animal about to pounce. Heat coiled in her womb and she felt moisture begin to seep from the juncture of her thighs.

"I'm like a wolf, Peaches," he growled, his voice low, almost frightening, "and you are my mate. If anyone thinks to take you from me, I will kill him and then have you on top of his bloody corpse."

Her head spun with the possibilities of being taken in such a ferocious manner by this beautiful man. His face was now so close to hers that if she'd but blink her eyelashes would tangle with his. Though he hadn't even touched her yet, she was sure her breathing shamelessly revealed her excitement.

Feeling to her toes that she truly was his mate, she leaned her head towards his and audibly inhaled his scent in the way a canine would. It was a blatant, primitively sexual invitation to him and she hoped he saw it that way. "Show me," she exhaled her evocative statement.

Chapter Eleven

Blood had rushed so quickly to Luke's cock he'd nearly popped his fly. He'd originally envisioned her naked and spread out before him like some sumptuous, heathen banquet, but her unashamed invitation to indulge in his fantasy made him push the sensual vision aside for the time being. The pounding beat of his pulse told him he needed to be inside that tight pussy of hers. And now he had her permission to fully unleash the beast within.

He let a low growl rumble in his throat and returned her inhalation with one of his own. He grazed his nose down the side of her neck as he took in her scent, sensing the unmistakable aroma of lust mixed with her own personal fragrance. He felt more than saw her shudder. Taking her by the shoulders, he laid her back upon his bedroll.

Digging into her layers of cotton with one hand and freeing himself with the other, he found what he was searching for. By the scent of her arousal, he could tell she was begging to become one with him. Stripping her bloomers from her legs, he sank himself into her sweet, warm cunt with a deep thrust of his hips. He was rewarded by her cry, which echoed off the walls of the shallow cave.

As he drove into her tight, wet heat again and again, scraping his lips and tongue across her skin, he clawed his hand at her through the hindering fabric, pretending to slash it from her body. He felt powerful—his devotion to his mate made him feel wild, dangerous. With his teeth he drew a ragged path up the side of her neck and he covered her ear with his mouth for another growl. As he did so, he felt her tremors begin—desperately undulating around him as he pounded into her, his rhythm driving and fierce, her passionate screams ringing in his head. God, he could fuck her forever. He rose up and watched her angelic mouth gasping for air in between her fervent cries as she came. His grin felt more like a satisfied baring of teeth.

Consumed by the storm of his lovemaking, he felt her pulling him back down to her by his neck, and suddenly he wanted to merge with her, to seep into her skin. He pressed his forehead to hers and began kissing her face, her neck, every exposed length of flesh he could reach.

Shit, she was coming again. He joined her, roaring his release.

Beatrice didn't want to move from underneath his weight. He'd loved her so thoroughly, so completely, she didn't care if she never walked again. And how wicked he'd been, pretending to be a wild animal—she grinned languidly. The first time he'd growled at her, she'd never wanted anything more in her entire life than to be taken by him, no matter how violently.

And now, here they were, melting into one another, satisfied on so many levels it should have been against the law.

"Did I frighten you?" he whispered.

Her ear tickled with his soft whisper. "Yes. And I loved it." Her voice held a satisfied femininity she hadn't known existed.

Beatrice felt his belly vibrating against her as he laughed. "Why, you little vixen."

She giggled. "Perhaps you should punish my waywardness."

Luke leaned up and rested his cheek on the palm of his hand. "I'm afraid you'd like it far too much to be considered a punishment."

Smiling, she lifted a weary limb and traced the hollow of his cheek with her finger. "Then perhaps you should think up another sort of punishment for me." Unable to hide the grin, she tucked her lower lip between her teeth.

"That can be arranged," he murmured just before his mouth swooped down to take hers in a deep kiss.

* * * *

In the cover of darkness, Luke had walked Beatrice to the edge of her property, kissed her goodbye, and left to go back to the cave.

She washed the hours of lovemaking from her skin with a cloth, while juicy lemon slices floated and bobbed in the warm water. Luke mentioned that he liked the way she smelt lemony, and she promised herself she'd make every effort to smell like citrus for him all the time. Donning her last clean nightdress, Beatrice then crawled into bed exhausted.

Luke was now farther away than he'd originally been, and she wasn't happy about it in the least. In order to keep from dwelling upon the sad subject, her mind hopped about as she tried to settle down and fall asleep.

Tomorrow she'd go to town and seek out Doc Holliday. This unjustified matter needed to be settled, and soon.

She'd never thought in her wildest dreams she'd have a lover. And to think—his very life was in danger since before he'd come to Tombstone. The unfair situation gave her good cause to try to right the wrong against him, and, by God, she'd do whatever it took.

Over an hour later, when she'd finally begun drifting off to sleep, she heard the soft patter of rain on the roof. Suddenly grateful that Luke was now under the shelter of the cave, she offered up a whispered prayer of thanks.

* * * *

It was as if Doc Holliday's name was in the air that had been refreshed by the light rain from the night before. On the way to see Mr McElroy and acquire information from him as to Holliday's whereabouts, Beatrice had found out that Doc and Kate Elder were staying at Fly's Boarding House. Changing directions, she headed towards Fly's, nervous as all outdoors about presenting her case to Doc.

Having been told the room number by the proprietor, Beatrice knocked on the door and waited. Someone in the building was having an awful coughing fit, but she disregarded it when the door opened.

"Can I help you?"

The woman who answered the door had to have been Kate Elder. She was of foreign extraction, European to be exact. Her reddish-brown hair leaned towards frizzy as little wisps escaped from her simple coif. Her unadorned day dress was of a fine lawn fabric in emerald green. She assessed Beatrice in the same fashion in which she was being surveyed.

Beatrice cleared her throat. "Hello. My name is Mrs Lindley Gaitland and I am looking for Doc Holliday."

With one more visual perusal from Beatrice's head to her toes, Miss Elder swung open the door for her to enter. It wasn't in a rude manner—it seemed more cautionary. "I am Kate Elder, and this"—she indicated with a sweep of her hand to an occupied chair next to an open window—"is Doc Holliday."

Miss Elder had done well with the English, Beatrice thought, having easily detected her Hungarian accent. With determination she set her gaze upon the man whom everyone was talking about. The breeze stirred the cream sheer curtains behind him, causing them to billow into the room.

He lit his cigarette, shook out the flame, and stood. "And whom do we have the pleasure of addressin'?"

"Forgive me," Miss Elder interjected, "this is Mrs Lindley Gaitland."

Doc took Beatrice's hand and bowed over it in a very gallant, Southern manner. "Charmed"—he returned to a seated position—"but I have a distinct feeling you're not here on some sort of social call."

Beatrice dipped her hand into her reticule and pulled out Luke's deck of cards. She set the cards on the table next to Doc.

Doc observed the deck and looked up at her, cocking an eyebrow.

"I'm sure I don't have to tell you why I'm here."

Doc took a hit from his cigarette. "No" — he blew out the smoke — "you must be here about Luke."

Beatrice nodded. "He's in trouble and I understand you may be able to help him. You see, Allen Gaitland, my late husband's brother, has put his nose where it doesn't belong. I have reason to believe he and a few other lawmen are after Luke for the stabbing of a Mr Davis."

"What can I do about it, Mrs Gaitland, when I half expect some trumped up charge to be brought to my door at any hour of the day?"

"Luke tells me you were there. He says you were witness to the scuffle. I suspect, if you were to testify on Luke's behalf, he could be freed of the charge."

Doc took another long draw. "He's told you the truth, ma'am." He expelled the smoke from his lungs and closely observed the cigarette between his fingers. "However, I am not disposed to walking into a courtroom unless bid by the authorities to do so."

"But, sir, he's had to go into hiding because of this incident — you're his only hope." Beatrice's voice trembled and her eyes stung as tears threatened to emerge.

Doc stood. "It was very nice makin' your acquaintance, ma'am." He bowed slightly. "I'll think on it." He turned and walked through a doorway that led out on to the balcony.

Feeling no surer about the situation than when she'd walked in, Beatrice turned towards the front door.

"Wait —" Miss Elder reached out and took Beatrice by the elbow. Beatrice turned to face her. "Is this Allen Gaitland the same man who goes by Al, and just got into town not two weeks ago?"

Beatrice thought for a moment. "I've never heard him go by Al, but he did get into town recently."

"Sandy-brown hair, about this tall?" Miss Elder held up her hand so that it hovered about three inches over her head.

Beatrice nodded.

"Well, Mrs Gaitland, I have some news which might offend your more delicate sensibilities."

The slow tattoo of Beatrice's heartbeat suddenly thudded loud and dull in her ears. Unable to form a single word, she nodded her encouragement for Miss Elder to continue.

"If it is in fact the same man, he's been frequenting my friend Dolly's bordello."

"No, not Allen." It was an impossibility. "How do you know?"

"I'd gone to Dolly's last night for a visit. From the parlour, I saw him enter a private room with one of the girls and then, not too long after, she left and another entered. Dolly told me Al was her most recent regular."

Beatrice faced the window. Her gaze settled on Doc's back as he stood on the balcony smoking another cigarette. Were all men alike? Did they all need to spend themselves in a scarlet woman at one time or another? First Lindley, now Allen. The thought made her stomach churn.

Jolted from her reverie when Miss Elder spoke again, Beatrice snapped her gaze to meet the woman's serious hazel-brown eyes. "I heard him say to one of the girls that he'd be back tomorrow night."

"Tonight?" Beatrice's voice was hollow and distant even to her own ears. Trying to bring herself back to the conversation at hand, she felt Miss Elder considering her for a moment.

"Don't you believe me?"

Beatrice turned back to Miss Elder. "It does seem a little far-fetched, don't you think? A newly arrived pastor visiting a house where...a lady's...affections are...negotiable?" She dismissed the annoying pauses between words as good manners in this indelicate situation—one certainly didn't just blurt things out of such a private nature.

"You'd be surprised at how many different types of men are disposed to do such."

"Do all men? Even after they are married?" A silent huff of air caught in Beatrice's throat as she was appalled that the thought had escaped her lips before she could stop it.

Miss Elder tipped her head as if thinking about her answer. "Some men visit, er, *boarding houses* before they are married. Some even carry on their appointments afterwards, if their wives aren't fulfilling their needs. But, in saying that, I will have to admit no, not all men continue after they are married."

If anyone knew of the carnal habits of men, it would be Miss Elder. It had been whispered that she was a working girl from time to time herself and, being such, Beatrice imagined that she frequented those circles with no amount of trepidation whatsoever.

"Are you still unconvinced it was your Allen Gaitland at Dolly's last night?"

Beatrice's answer was a shrug of a shoulder. A 'yes' would blindly implicate Allen and a 'no' would call Miss Elder a liar.

"I can arrange for you to catch him in the act, if you wish."

Beatrice stared unseeing for a moment while her mind flashed back to the awful night of her husband's death, when that horrid woman's presence had become known to Beatrice by accident. "Will *she* be there?" she asked, forcing down a lump of emotion in her throat. "That filthy pink woman?"

A flash of anger sparked in Miss Elder's eyes that didn't go unnoticed by Beatrice. "They used to call her Pinky, but one night she went into Dolly's hat box and took the house's money. From that night on the girls referred to her as Pinky-Pig. All of them, including Dolly, have made a vow that if she ever shows her face again they will butcher her into chops."

Despite the brutal visual, Beatrice's shoulders relaxed.

Miss Elder reached out and patted her hand. "She won't be coming back. It was said that she often slept with men for alcohol, laudanum, absinthe—she was a desperate addict and a bad one at that. I heard they used to make fun of her behind her back. Apparently she couldn't hold the liquor she so anxiously sought. Dolly says Pinky-Pig will likely drink away the hundreds of dollars she's stolen."

Shuddering, Beatrice uttered, "What a sad, lost soul."

Miss Elder agreed with a nod. "Just so she stays lost."

Then there was the situation with Allen. Something had to be done, even if it was punishment by public humiliation. She raised her chin a notch and looked Miss Elder square in the eyes. "How can we go about catching Allen red-handed?"

A slow smile lifted the corners of Miss Elder's lips. "I have an idea, but it will take some courage on your part."

"Tell me." Beatrice pushed away a tremor of warning to the back corner of her mind.

Miss Elder took a few steps away from Beatrice and turned back, assessing her the way she had when she'd first arrived. "I will provide a disguise for you and we'll set you up at Dolly's."

Beatrice's lungs constricted for a moment, as she was unable to believe that Miss Elder would propose such a scandalous event. She'd never thought in her lifetime she'd be asked to step foot in a bordello. Beatrice began to shake her head when Miss Elder spoke.

"I will see to the secrecy of your identity and your safety, on that you may rest assured."

Miss Elder seemed so very sincere. Beatrice glanced over at the door and observed Doc as he leaned against the portal listening. If she agreed to Miss Elder's plan, would Doc be more inclined to help Luke? She swallowed her fear, which had created a lump in her throat, and nodded in agreement.

Miss Elder smiled. "Good. Meet me behind the Shepherd of the Hills tent at sundown."

After expressing her thanks and sliding one more glance at Doc, Beatrice quit the room.

Kate watched as Doc finished rolling a new cigarette. When he finished, he turned to face her. "You are a wicked woman, indeed."

"What makes you say so?"

"How will you vouch for that woman's safety, not to mention the privacy of her person?"

"Don't be ridiculous. Dolly always takes care of her own." She made to walk away from him when he caught her by the elbow.

"Mrs Gaitland is not one of Dolly's girls."

"I will work it out—there is no need to fuss."

Angry, Doc began to dig his fingers into her arm, but he held himself in check this time. Too many nights they'd disagree about one thing or another, threatening more than just bodily harm. And, each instance, everyone within the walls of the boarding house was witness to their volatile arguments. "You are putting that young woman in danger, Kate. You should have asked for my help. You can't possibly do this on your own."

"Your help? You didn't seem so keen to help that poor boy—and that nice woman came all the way down here to ask you for assistance."

"That's different."

"No it's not. Look, why don't you just mind your own fucking business," she snapped.

"It *is* my business. Luke happens to be one of the very few people on this godforsaken planet with whom I get along."

She tried to pull away from him. "Then why won't you help him out of his situation when you know he'd do the same for you in a heartbeat?"

With a growl, Doc threw her arm from his grasp and went to the sideboard to pour himself a shot of whisky. He tossed it back then slammed the glass down.

Doc didn't look up when she placed the deck of cards Mrs Gaitland had left next to his fist.

Chapter Twelve

Beatrice had been waiting there for nearly ten minutes and had almost fled the scene three times when Miss Elder came around the corner of the tent.

"Thank the Lord," Beatrice murmured then almost laughed about God being thanked that the woman had shown up to take her to a house of iniquity.

"Take your clothes off," Miss Elder said, as if it were a normal thing to say in conversation.

"What?" Beatrice nearly shrieked.

"You can't very well go over in your widow's weeds. You will be recognised."

Beatrice looked down at her clothes. "Oh," she said feebly, and began fussing with the ties and hooks.

"Here, let me help."

In no time, Beatrice stood shivering in her underpinnings, but not because of the weather.

Miss Elder stepped back and shook her head. "Those are far too clean. Take them off."

Beatrice was horrified that Miss Elder would suggest such. "Am I to walk about unclothed?"

Smiling, Miss Elder opened her black and white striped carpet bag. "Of course not. Here." She reached into the bag and held up a pair of dingy bloomers, a frayed corset, and a sheer robe. "They're stained but freshly laundered."

Beatrice slid her own bloomers to her ankles and tossed them at Miss Elder's feet, unhooked the front of her corset, allowing it to fall to the ground, and stood in her stockings and shoes with her hand out, waiting for Miss Elder to dispense to her the disguise. To her great mortification, Miss Elder was smiling as she assessed her.

"You have twenty-dollar thighs, Mrs Gaitland."

At once Beatrice raised her arms to cover her body. "What?"

"Each," Miss Elder grinned. "If you ever find yourself in a financial crush, I can settle you into the profession in no time."

Timidly stretching out a hand, Beatrice silently asked Miss Elder for the other clothes pieces. Covering her body as quickly as possible, she murmured her thanks. "As much as I appreciate the offer, I must decline."

Miss Elder laced her into the corset, and, moments later, Beatrice tied the robe closed, looking to her co-conspirator for approval.

"Your hair," Miss Elder murmured as she stuffed Beatrice's other clothes into her carpet bag.

Raising her hand and patting it into place Beatrice asked, "What, is it in a shambles?"

Miss Elder pressed her lips together then crooked a finger at Beatrice. When Beatrice stepped forward, Miss Elder began pulling the pins from the coif, letting it fall to swing freely around Beatrice's shoulders and hips.

"Are you sure this is advisable?" Beatrice fisted her hands, her palms itching to collect the fly-away tresses back into a loose knot.

"With your hair like this I can *guarantee* you won't be recognised as we head over to Dolly's."

Beatrice nodded, and Miss Elder stood back to appraise her work. "Perfect. You would indeed fetch a great price. Don't overlook my offer."

"How could I ever forget such?" Beatrice said in a small voice.

Snatching up her now overstuffed carpet bag, Miss Elder took Beatrice in an indirect route to Dolly's. As they walked along, Beatrice had many questions that were nagging to be asked. She glanced at Miss Elder several times to voice her enquiries, but couldn't muster up the courage.

After about the fifth time, Miss Elder looked at Beatrice. "You seem as if you want to say something."

"Er—" Beatrice cleared her throat. "Miss Elder, there are things I'm curious about, things I have no business asking, and yet I find myself dwelling upon finding the elusive answers. Would you be offended were I to ask you a few things?"

"First, I'd like for you to call me Kate, and second, if you will not be offended by my replies, I promise not to be shocked by your questions." Kate grinned, which put Beatrice mightily at ease.

"Then you should call me Beatrice."

Kate agreed with a decisive nod. "Go on, then."

"Do—" Beatrice swallowed, her cheeks aflame. "Do the girls like what they do?"

Thankfully, Kate looked as if she knew exactly what she was talking about, because there was no way Beatrice would have been able to explain herself.

"It all depends upon the john."

"The john being the—the customer?"

"Precisely. The girls are there to make a living, and don't have the luxury of picking and choosing between men. Of course, if someone like you were to get into the trade—"

"Thank you again, but that's not likely to happen."

Kate snorted, but Beatrice ignored it.

"What do these johns do?"

"Well, some come in already hard and wanting a poke or two. Others need encouragement."

"Encouragement?"

"As in a bit of fondling and stroking, you know, to get their pricks ready for sport. Some customers just want to be sucked on 'till they find their fulfilment." Kate gaze met Beatrice's as if assessing how she was taking the news. After a moment, she continued. "Then there are the men that only want to watch."

"W—watch?"

"Mmm-hmm. And then there are the ones who want to be restrained or spanked...or both."

Swallowing a strangled choke, Beatrice felt the heat of her blush from head to toe, but, before she could comment, Kate continued. "It's not all that bad. Sometimes there will be a clean-smelling man, with a rifle between his legs as opposed to a pocket pistol, who has the urge to satisfy as well as be satisfied. That's the man who gets all the attention. The girls see a man like him come in and prices drop lower than necklines."

Beatrice would have laughed at Kate's narrative, but her nerves prohibited such frivolity. Her feet felt heavy, as if lead had been laid inside her shoes. Beatrice couldn't believe she was willingly going into a house where—

"Here we are," Kate announced as she guided Beatrice inside.

Beatrice hadn't known what to expect, perhaps a lightning bolt from above, but nothing of the sort happened. The parlour was a bit gaudy, if not richly done for a mining camp bordello. Thick red velvet paper covered the walls—their columned, floral designs begged to be stroked. Shaded candle lights winked from beneath coloured etched-glass globes. There were many chairs and settees covered in plush velvet fabrics, and the windows had heavy fringed curtains drawn over them. A few girls were lounging around waiting for their johns.

Beatrice was suddenly glad she had asked Kate her questions and, moreover, relieved that Kate had answered her without being shocked that the enquiries had come from a pastor's wife.

From around a corner, a well-dressed woman came and stood next to Kate and nodded her greeting after looking Beatrice up and down in the same manner Kate had. "Al ain't here yet, Kate, but someone else's been waiting for the woman you were to arrive with. He wouldn't have no other girl. Even when they offered several free tumbles, he refused."

Beatrice gasped, her heart seemingly in her throat. "Someone knows I'm here?" She watched as Dolly whispered something in Kate's ear.

Kate turned and grinned at Beatrice. "Come." Kate took her by the elbow and down a corridor, while Dolly tittered behind them, her laughter echoing in the parlour.

"Where are we going?" she asked, her voice squeezed from her throat unsteadily.

"You'll see."

Terrified, Beatrice was pushed into a pitch-black room. The door slammed shut behind her. She could hear fabric rustling from across the void of darkness. Holding her breath, she tried to ascertain if Kate had just tossed her into a room where people were fornicating.

A match struck, the sparks dying before the flame took to the candle wick.

Sweet Jesus, it was Luke. Her shoulders relaxed and she exhaled with relief.

Splayed casually across a fainting couch in his shirtsleeves and drawers, Luke took up a deck of cards and began shuffling.

Beatrice recognised the cards to be the ones she'd left at Doc's. "I see you've spoken to Doc." She tilted her head towards the deck in his hands.

He nodded. "But let's not talk of that now." He grinned in the dim golden light. "You wanna play a game, Peaches?"

Her heart began to pound and her throat went dry. Knowing the type of place they were in, and the state of Luke's undress, she doubted he was speaking of bezique.

"What kind of game?" Her query came out in a breathy whisper. So much for her attempt to sound brave.

"Why don't you take off that robe and we'll talk about it."

Luke was so handsome, so manly. It was no wonder the girls were offering themselves to him in exchange for nothing. Suddenly, she felt flattered that he wanted only her. A tremulous grin lifted the corners of her mouth and she untied her robe, letting it fall to the ground.

Luke eyed her from head to toe and back again. A low sound of approval came from his throat that caused the very room to tilt. "We are going to make believe I've paid for your services."

She heard her own breath catch in her throat and she shivered a little as chills ran over her body. She nodded, not trusting her own voice.

"You are mine now, my dove. I can do any manner of things to you, because I've paid for the right."

She nodded again, her insides turning molten.

"As such, I want you to remove your clothes. Very slowly."

She turned away from him. *I can do this,* she egged herself on. *He's already seen my body. Playing along won't be such a chore.* She then noticed a lock on the door. She reached up and slid the bolt home. The knowledge that they were behind a locked door seemed to give her just the amount of courage she needed.

Turning back to Luke, she took her time untying the waist of her bloomers, letting them slide down her legs. She then kicked off her shoes along with the bloomers.

Luke's gaze landed on the juncture of her thighs.

She felt hot moisture gather there that threatened to ooze down between her legs.

"So beautiful." He licked his lips.

Her knees felt as weak as if they were made of water.

"The corset next."

She undid the busk one hook at a time, until the garment fell away from her skin.

Hearing his breath hitch, she made to remove her stockings.

"No, leave those."

Luke set his deck down and stood, holding a steadying hand out to her.

She took his hand and he led her to the bed. "Lay down," he commanded, his voice soft.

She watched as he reached for and undid one of the pretty red bows attached to either side of the brass headboard. Almost protesting his action, she was interrupted when Luke lifted one of her hands up to meet the thick satin ribbon. He pressed her hand to the pole in a silent gesture to keep it there. He wrapped the ribbon around her wrist a few times and finally tied off the bow.

"Luke—"

"You trust me, don't you, sweetheart?" he asked tenderly.

At her nod, he did the same for her other wrist. He then lifted her hair from her chest and set it on the silk-covered pillow behind her.

Her heart pounded, her cheeks were on fire, her body was unclothed, vulnerable, open.

She watched him caress her body with his gaze.

He slid his languid, hungry stare from between her legs to her face.

Her longing to know what he was thinking all but stole her breath away.

"Uncomfortable, still?" He didn't wait for her answer. "I can fix that."

Luke bent over and pulled her robe from the floor. He removed the wide sash and sat next to her on the bed.

"Trust me, all right?" At her nod he crooked his finger at her face.

Unable to guess what he aspired to do with the strip of satin, Beatrice raised her head from the pillow.

"Close your eyes. I won't hurt you."

Her eyes fluttered shut. She felt the sash fall across her eyes, then Luke secured it behind her head. He placed his hands on either side of her face and, after kissing each cheek, he lowered her head to the pillow.

The blood rushing through her body was so amplified she could hear it above her own rapid breathing. Her lips sought moisture and she folded them in to meet the tip of her tongue.

After a rustling of fabric that she could only deduce was the rest of his clothes being removed, the mattress dipped as he sat next to her on the bed. At once she became aware of the weight of her breasts. She needed him to cover them, to lean his warm chest to hers, to knead them as he had done to her bottom when he'd hidden under her skirts. Her nipples puckered tightly and tingled as she gasped in eager expectation.

"Now" — he stroked his hands down her arms — "if at any time you feel frightened, tell me so and I'll stop."

Oh, she was frightened all right, but couldn't get herself to confess. "Just — just keep talking to me. Let me know you're there."

"All right, sweetheart."

"W — what are you going to do?"

She felt his lips graze her cheek. "Pleasure you," he whispered.

Beatrice shivered at the sound and feel of his words across her skin. Luke was a master at orchestrating sensations in her, but being blindfolded and restrained added multiple layers to her awareness, and an anticipation she'd never thought possible. But, still, she couldn't have done this with someone whom she didn't trust.

She felt his lips kiss a route from just below her ear to her chest, but he spoke quietly as he did so. "I've only done this one other time." His tongue flicked out to tease one of her nipples. His big, warm hands cupped her aching breasts and she inhaled long and deep.

His hands on her body were exactly what she needed. Beatrice quivered and moaned softly, her sensitivity causing her to feel as fragile as a hundred-year-old teacup.

"However, I was the one bound to the bed." He chuckled as if embarrassed by his admittance.

"Did you enjoy it?" She squeaked with pleasure as he toyed with her other nipple.

She felt Luke's hand slide between her breasts and pause. "It was like nothing else in the world." His voice husky, as he recalled the ecstasy. With that, his hand stroked all the way down her belly.

Desperate for more contact, she lifted her hips, offering herself to him, her knees rubbing against each other seeking any sensation she could rally. Lord, but she was wet between her legs.

"You're a saucy one," his voice rumbled, blowing over her skin like a hot breeze that sent more waves of gooseflesh across her body.

Squirming against her bonds, Beatrice could hear the smile in his voice. "Luke..." His name tumbled from her lips in the barest of whispers.

The weight of the mattress shifted and Beatrice felt her legs being parted so that her ankles dropped to either side of the mattress.

"Now, what I'm about to do," he said as he settled himself between her legs, "requires my mouth. So it's going to be a little bit difficult to speak." He chuckled in a most wicked manner. "But I shall do my very best."

Beatrice drew in a breath to enquire further, but it froze in her throat as he began placing kisses over the mound of flesh between her legs. More moisture seeped towards her opening. Slowly Beatrice's hips tilted up, pressing against his face as if seeking more kisses — harder kisses.

He growled and suddenly his mouth came down on her, separating the folds of her flesh, adding the wetness of his tongue to her already soaked womanhood.

She sighed, thinking she was going to die from the ultimate pleasure of his naughty attentions.

When his fingers joined his lips and took over holding her open, she cursed aloud.

"Oh yes, you like this," he murmured against her.

Absolute understatement.

His tongue licked her as if she were a sweet from a candy jar. She'd never felt anything so exquisite in her entire life. His lips closed around her and he moaned, the sound reverberating through her whole body. When he began to suck on her, she knew her episode was going to be the grandest she'd ever experienced.

His hands slipped under her bottom and he raised her hips. She felt as if she were being offered up for sacrifice.

She panted and gasped as he drew her in and out again, over and over until she sang out her conclusion loud and long. He denied her a respite until she was so frenzied she could no longer stand to have his mouth on her. She tried to squirm away but he held her there, pressing his tongue against her sensitive flesh.

Beatrice sobbed his name and he finally lowered her hips to the bed. However, before she could form a coherent thought, he plunged into her. Her insides rebelled pleasurably against the intrusion, squeezing and undulating with every surge of his hard, demanding manhood.

"Come, my sweet little trollop," Luke said through clenched teeth as he rammed into her. "Tell me you love it. Tell me you want more and you want it hard."

"Yes," her voice was shrill in her own ears as she answered him, "take me harder. I want you to."

"You're a wayward little priss, so sweet and wet."

Suddenly, Beatrice felt Luke's hand slide between their bodies and his fingers began toying once again with her sensitised nub, manipulating it up and down, matching the rhythm of his body.

She held her breath as another wave was about to crash over her.

"Yes, that's it," he groaned. "Come with me now."

They both cried out in violent passion as their bodies climaxed, long, intense, shattering exquisitely. Repeated convulsions shuddered their muscles until, finally, all went quiet and they lay there sated, their breathing the only sound in the room.

Luke reached up and lifted the blindfold from her eyes. She blinked. The room seemed brighter than it had been before. He then untied her hands and set them, one by one, carefully upon her chest. Her arms ached, as did her entire body, but she didn't protest. He brought her feet back onto the bed, then gathered her body tenderly to his, settling with her on the narrow bed.

"That was…" she began when she found her voice, but was unable to find the right phrase.

"I know." Luke hugged her close. "It was for me, too."

A serene smile warmed her heart as she drifted off to a dreamless sleep.

Chapter Thirteen

"Beatrice Victoria Hughson," Luke whispered, seeing how the name would feel on his lips. "Delightful." He grinned.

He knew down deep the fantasy was fruitless. It wasn't likely he'd be cleared of the murder charge — the world didn't always work in the favour of the innocent. But, if God would smile on him and things did work out, he'd take Beatrice away from this bowl of dust, back to the East Coast where life was civilised, and marry her. He'd put her in fancy clothes and place her in the parlours of good society where all the women would adore her witty personality and all the men would envy him for having such an agreeable, beautiful wife. And if word ever got out that he and his wife spent hours in the bedroom doing God only knew what, and enjoyed doing so, the tongues would surely wag.

If truth be told, he wouldn't accept a stack of hundred-dollar chips to hear what everyone else thought, but he knew without a doubt she'd outshine them all and he'd be proud to have her on his arm as Mrs Lucas Hughson.

He kissed the top of her head and smiled.

She was no delicate flower, though. She'd probably start clubs and head up different societies, throw grand cotillions and entertaining garden parties — which was exactly what she should be doing, not drying up like a tumbleweed in this harsh desert climate.

Luke rubbed his cheek on her sweet-scented hair.

She stirred then sat up with a gasp. "I can't believe I fell asleep. What time is it?"

The sound of her soft, feminine voice tickled his ears and sent blood rushing to his extremities. God, but he could have gone for another round if they had the time. "Must be getting close to ten."

"What will we do if Allen doesn't show up?" She looked at him, her eyes wide with something akin to innocence, but he knew better.

"Oh, I'm sure I could think of something," he drawled.

Before she could respond, a soft knock sounded at the door. "He's on his way," came a voice from the hall.

Luke didn't reply, but hugged Beatrice once more. "And now for the less pleasurable part of the evening," he murmured.

Reluctantly, Luke got up and handed Beatrice her discarded items. He dressed as well.

When they emerged from the room, Dolly told them that Kate had been the one to alert her to Al's pending arrival and that, not wishing to be present for the disclosure, Kate had returned to Fly's to retire with Doc for the evening.

Dolly instructed a few of the girls to hang about the parlour and distract Al any way they could when he came in.

Beatrice and Luke had their heads together in the doorway to Dolly's office.

"I don't want Allen to see you when he comes in, Luke." She indicated to the front door with a jab of her thumb over her shoulder. "He'll have recognised you on the poster by now and will try his hand at enforcing the law."

"Don't you worry about me, sweetheart. I'll—"

Just then the door to the brothel swung open.

Luke ducked down and peered over her shoulder. "It's him," he whispered.

Beatrice felt her eyes go wide—her feet seemed frozen to the ground. "What do I do?"

Dolly was sitting on a well-cushioned seat behind her desk and had obviously heard the quiet exchange. Jumping up, she whispered, "All right, now you've seen him. Leave through the tunnel. This way." She blew the flame out from a lamp, which sat on the corner of her desk, then stepped over to open the trapdoor.

Luke took Beatrice's hand to draw her into the dark office when Allen spoke from behind her.

"I don't remember seeing you here. You're new, aren't you?"

The air left Beatrice's lungs in a silent whoosh. "Go," she mouthed and shooed at Luke with one hand.

Before Beatrice could turn around to answer Allen, she felt him pick up a lock of her hair. "I hope you are not too expensive." He sniffed. "But then again," he chuckled, "I just might pay any price for a tumble with you."

Luke swooped forward like an avenging angel. "You'll be dead before you open your fly."

Allen released Beatrice's hair and shoved an accusing finger in Luke's face. "You!"

Beatrice turned to put herself between Allen and Luke, her survival instincts prompting her to shove Allen as far away from Luke as possible.

Caught off guard, Allen stumbled backwards, knocking over a small table in the process, and landed on his rump. His eyes were wide as he looked Beatrice up and down from his position on the floor. "My God, Beatrice?"

Luke grabbed Beatrice by the waist and hoisted her off her feet. He slammed the door to Dolly's office, cutting off Allen's view, and shoved the bolt home.

"Over here!" Dolly said from behind a privacy screen.

Luke took Beatrice to where Dolly held open the trapdoor. "Thanks, Dolly. I owe you."

"Go on then, and take your fine lady with you. Hurry now."

After helping Beatrice down, Luke paused just before she shut the door over them. "Will you be all right, Dolly?"

Retrieving a small gun from her cleavage, Dolly answered, giving it a wave. "Me and my derringer will be just fine. Now go!"

The door shut and Beatrice and Luke found themselves surrounded by a thick blackness. Luke struck a match. "This way." He indicated with the small light in his hand down the dirt corridor.

"Your matches have come in handy tonight. Where did you get them?"

Luke grabbed her hand. "Won 'em from Doc." He grinned just before pulling her down the tunnel.

They made their way quickly through the twisting passageway until it finally sloped up and came out of the ground amongst some thick brush behind a Chinese laundry.

Luke helped her out of the tunnel. "You know you can't go home, Allen will be waiting for you."

Beatrice gasped. She hadn't thought of that. "What do I—? Where do I—?"

Luke took her in his arms. "Shh, it will be all right. I'll take you back to the cave. Will that be agreeable?"

She nodded against his neck then looked up at him. "As long as you are with me, anywhere will do."

Luke's heart constricted—her voice, strong with conviction, reverberated to his very soul. He knew she needed him even though she might not admit it out loud. It felt good, right, as if all was as it should be. Too bad it was only an improbable fantasy. If God could see fit to grant him more time with her, he'd protect her with his life, forever. "Come on." He released her and took her hand to lead her towards the Dragoon Mountains.

Once they'd made it back to the cave, Luke did his best to adjust the bedroll so that it would accommodate two.

With moonlight washing over her from behind, Beatrice stood at the entrance, her arms wrapped around her middle, still visibly shaken from their flight. "How on earth did this get out of hand so quickly?" she murmured.

Luke looked up. "Sweetheart, you should come away from there."

"Why?" she asked as she turned to look at him.

The sound of a gun cocking echoed loudly in the shallow cave. "Because, you stupid slut, someone might see you in your fancy underpinnings."

Luke shot to his feet. *Shit*. The bastard had followed them.

"Come on, Hughson, I dare you," Allen taunted.

"Gaitland, take the gun off Beatrice, for God's sake. She's a lady."

Allen chuckled. "Really? None of the ladies I know dress like this in public." Then he added through clenched teeth, "Unless they're advertising their wares."

Luke looked around for a weapon.

"Try it and she'll have a hole in her head bigger than the one between her legs."

Beatrice gasped at his crude words.

"Gaitland, I'll not have you speaking in such a vulgar manner in front of Beatrice."

"Shut up, Hughson," Allen snapped, then sobered. "I'm the one with the gun, I'll make the rules," he drawled as if his remark was something one heard in everyday conversation.

Still at the wrong end of Allen's gun, Beatrice spoke. "What do you want, Allen. Money? Property?"

"What I want from you will come later, but, for right now, I'm taking you both in."

"She's done nothing wrong, Gaitland. Let her go."

"Harbouring a fugitive of the law isn't wrong? Oh, yes, that's right. You don't think murder is wrong either, do you, Hughson?"

"Luke is innocent, Allen." Beatrice's shaking voice made Luke want to run to her.

Allen grabbed Beatrice by the arm. "So sayeth the minister's wife who works part-time at a whore house. You know, Beatrice, I'd have paid you to drop your bloomers for me. You didn't have to resort to strangers and degenerates."

Luke took a menacing step towards Allen.

"Don't do it," Allen warned.

Luke's gaze locked with Beatrice's.

"All right. Let's go. Both of you keep your hands where I can see them. Hughson, you lead the way directly to the sheriff's office." Once Luke was out of the cave he watched over his shoulder as Allen guided Beatrice along the path. "And don't do anything stupid, Hughson. You already have one murder on your hands."

No one said a word as they slowly made their way to town.

The town marshal was not in when they arrived at the office, but a new deputy, whom Beatrice hadn't seen before, helped Allen incarcerate she and Luke into separate cells.

When the deputy departed for the office and Allen was about to leave, he turned back to Beatrice. "I'll see you soon." He blew her a kiss.

Beatrice recoiled against the back wall. Luke growled and lunged at Allen, slamming into the bars of his cell.

Allen's laugh could be heard until the front door to the office shut out the annoying noise.

"I can't believe this is happening." Beatrice choked on a sob.

Luke went to her and held out his hands through the bars that separated them. "I'm so sorry you've been dragged into my affairs."

His voice was pained and it just about broke her heart. Stepping over and taking Luke's hands, she pressed herself against the cold iron, touching every part of him she could. She felt much better when his arms wrapped around her—even through the bars. "You don't have to apologise. We'll get this whole thing straightened out, I promise."

"I can't hold you to that promise, Peaches," he whispered as he stroked her hair.

She lifted her head and spoke with conviction. "But you are innocent!"

Luke cupped her jaw and stroked a thumb down her cheek. "We know that, but the populous doesn't. If we can't provide proof, then—"

"No, don't say it. I can't bear to hear the words." She sobbed.

"Oh, sweetheart." He hugged her despite the obstruction.

They held each other thus for a while, until Luke suggested they push the cots together on either side of the bars.

Through the night, despite Luke's soothing words and the comfort of his presence, she couldn't help but cry instead of sleep. But it wasn't pity for herself that caused her despair—it was Luke's plight. The world could be so cruel.

Even before the sun rose, Beatrice heard the voice of Marshal White in the office as his shift began. He and his wife had been regular attendees at Shepherd of the Hills ever since she and Lindley began their ministry in Tombstone. For months after Lindley's death, the Whites had had her over for meals at least twice a week. Marshal White was a kind, elderly man with white hair and a short beard to match. She couldn't see him as having the tough disposition it took to do the job he did, but she'd heard tell he did it well.

As she thought he might, Marshal White came bursting through the door. She rolled away from Luke and they rose to greet him.

"Mrs Gaitland! I came in the second I read the report." The marshal looked her up and down as if considering her state of undress. He went back into the office and quickly returned with a duster over his arm. "Gracious, you don't belong in there." He took an iron ring from the wall just outside the door and began fumbling with the keys.

"Thank you so much, Marshal. My friend Luke here is innocent. He doesn't belong—"

Marshal White paused and looked into her eyes. "I'm sorry, Mrs Gaitland. I can only let you go, not your friend." He opened the door for Beatrice and placed the duster over her shoulders.

She thanked him and turned to face Luke's cell. "But, as I said, he is innocent—"

"I would take your word for it in a second, my dear, but there is a price on his head. If I let him out, who knows what would befall him?"

Beatrice deflated some. The marshal was right. Luke would be safer from his enemies in jail.

Luke spoke up. "Sir?"

"Yes, son?"

"I have reason to believe someone is going to try to hurt Mrs Gaitland. Is there a way to protect her after she leaves here?"

"The only protection I can legally give is if she comes and files a complaint against the individual who violated her person or her property."

"You mean after the fact?" Luke asked incredulously. "But Marshal—"

Beatrice raised her hand and rested it upon a bar of Luke's cell to stop his protest. "There will be no need, for I will be spending as much of my time here with you as possible."

"I will be happy to accommodate for your safety, Mrs Gaitland," the marshal said sincerely and turned for the office. "I'll be in here when you are ready to leave," he murmured and shut the door.

"Beatrice," Luke began quietly, taking her by the hand.

She interrupted his speech. "Where else am I to go? Back to my cottage so that when Allen needs a maid, or whatever else he has in mind, I'll be there for him?" She pressed herself against the cell door. "I want to be with you."

A slight grin lifted one corner of his lips. "I suppose there would be no point in arguing with you."

"Smart man." However, her gumption was belied by her shaking voice.

Luke curled his arms around her waist, pulling her to him, ignoring the bars. "Then will you spend the rest of your life with me?"

Beatrice nodded and rested her head on the iron door, silently damning the impediment.

"Will you spend the rest of *my* life with me?"

She sucked in an involuntary gasp and looked up into his eyes. "It won't do at all to have you making morbid jokes at a time like this."

"I'm not joking," he murmured, despite his chuckling. He sobered then. "Will you marry me?"

She stared at him for a moment, then a sly grin curved her lips. "Shall I call the pastor?"

Luke laughed softly. "Now who's making morbid jokes?"

She lifted an innocent shoulder and he laughed in earnest.

Shaking her head as if to clear her mind, Beatrice rose up on to her toes to offer him her lips—her heart—her soul. "Yes, I will marry you." His mouth was cool against hers.

He ended the kiss. "God willing, I'll take you back home and marry you. How does that sound?"

Beatrice didn't want to think about the future, but nodded her acquiescence regardless.

"Now go get changed and come back when you can. Be very careful not to be alone. Keep to the busy streets. Allen will be less inclined to molest you while others are about."

Beatrice nodded again. "I'll be back as soon as I can." She gazed into his eyes once more. "What about you? I'm so worried—"

"Don't. I'll be fine. It's been a while since I had a roof over my head and a mattress under my back."

"You make jail sound like the Grand Hotel."

Giving Beatrice one more soft kiss, Luke released her and she left the marshal's office.

Beatrice made it to her cottage without incident. However, upon her arrival she discovered that her front door had been left ajar.

Someone was within. Her heart raced at the thought of the intruder being Allen. Silently she pushed open the door. Not a sound came from the parlour, so the trespasser must have been deeper inside the house.

She debated with herself whether she should proceed or not. Glancing down between the open duster, she viewed her soiled dove underpinnings from the night before. Beatrice had no choice—it was imperative that she go in, if only to avoid being seen by the townsfolk.

Beatrice quietly stepped inside, leaving the door open in case she needed to make a hasty exit.

Slowly she made her way past the kitchen. No one.
She let out a breath and drew in a new one.
At the end of the hallway loomed her bedroom.

Chapter Fourteen

A silent sigh passed between Beatrice's lips as she stepped towards her room. Her heart thudded against her ribs and her lungs burnt, demanding that she drag in another breath. Powerless to deny her body's request, she did so, but the rush of air in her throat sounded like a wind storm.

Focusing on the door before her, which was also left partly open, she waited, listening.

Silence met her straining ears.

She leaned closer and peered in through the crack.

Her bedcovers were in a jumble, as if someone had slept in them. She was positive she'd made the bed the day before—doing so was part of her morning routine.

Ignoring her pounding pulse, she steeled herself, and pushed open the door, thankful that she'd used her old armoire for firewood after Lindley had died.

It appeared she was the only person present. As the reality hit, she heaved a great sigh of relief.

Stepping towards the bed, she noticed the sheets. They were soiled. It was apparent that the person who had used them the night before had done so with their dirt-encrusted boots on.

As she looked more closely, she observed other sorts of stains and dried fluids, which made her stomach churn.

What sort of sick person would defile someone's privacy in this way?

Deftly, she divested the mattress of the filthy sheets and tossed them into the corner. She found the pillow on the floor — thankfully, it had not been soiled. She changed the casing, hoping to take it to Luke, along with what food she could gather from her kitchen.

* * * *

"Ah, Marshal White." Allen came through the door of the office, accompanied by a smug feeling that he was sure showed on his face. Normally he had to be judicious about allowing his emotions to be displayed, but he figured it was warranted, owing to his productive activities in the name of justice the night before. That, and the memory of where he'd slept — and in whose sheets he'd spent himself several times — made him feel like a satisfied stud horse. "I was hoping to find you here. What do think of the job I did last night in rounding up the criminals?"

The marshal looked up from his paperwork. "Pastor Allen, your indiscretion regarding Mrs Gaitland will be overlooked, but only because you brought in Lucas Hughson."

He started. "Wha — ?"

Marshal White held up a hand. "I don't have time to discuss this with you right now. I've got to send out these wires to get Mr Hughson's trial on the books. Now if you will excuse me?"

Allen made to protest but thought better of it. "I expect the reward money will be wired to my account soon?" His question was more of a statement, but he didn't care. When Marshal White didn't respond, Allen turned towards the open door that separated the incarcerated from the office. "I'll just pay a short visit to our prisoners."

From behind him, Allen heard the marshal's voice issue a curt command. "Keep that door open."

Reluctantly, Allen released the door he'd been about to shut, but relaxed and once again took up his smug attitude as he found Luke prostrate on his tiny cot, locked within the cage.

"So, where is your little playmate? Housing her in a different jail, are they?"

Luke's eyes opened halfway, then closed. "Marshal White let Beatrice go."

"What?" Allen nearly shouted.

"Are you going deaf?" Luke drawled. "You seem to be asking people to repeat themselves an awful lot."

In three strides Allen had reached the cell, and he pressed his body against the bars, his teeth gritted together in anger. "You little bastard, where is your whore?"

Luke shot to his feet. "Don't you dare call Beatrice a whore." He reached through the bars to grab his adversary but Allen stepped back, avoiding the threat. Instead, Luke took hold of the bars, his knuckles white with the intense grip. "Beatrice is a woman to be cherished and loved, not ordered around like a dog."

Allen chuckled. "When she becomes my wife, I will handle her as I see fit."

Luke released the bars. "She won't marry you, Gaitland," he murmured, a relaxed smile displaying his cockiness.

"You stupid boy. Just because you've been sniffing up her skirts, you think she's going to marry you?" He didn't allow Luke to respond. "You are a dead man."

"It doesn't matter. Neither do you matter. I know who she loves, and it's not you."

Allen would have given up a night at a whore house to get his hands around Luke's neck for five minutes. He relaxed. This kid would not get the best of him. "The very day you hang will be the day I make Beatrice my wife."

"It won't happen, Gaitland."

"Perhaps I'll marry her today," Allen looked Luke up and down and grinned. He lowered his voice so that only Luke could hear. "And when I get a hold of her, I'll burn more than just her porch."

Luke took a step towards Allen. "Leave her alone, you son of a bitch," he warned.

Allen licked his lips in anticipation. "I think I'll bend her over and take her in the ass."

Luke leapt for the bars. "God damn you, Gaitland! Don't you dare touch her!"

"That's enough!" Marshal White's voice barked from the door and both men looked up as he spoke. "If anything happens to Mrs Gaitland, you will be the first one I come after." The marshal ended with an index finger pointed directly at Allen's face.

A frozen moment hung in the air between the two men until the marshal waved Allen away. "Now get on out of here. There'll be no need for you to come back, either."

* * * *

Dressed in a simple, dark blue, linen gown, Beatrice hurried over to the Clarks', hoping to speak with Ginny.

She knocked, and, by the mercy of God, Ginny answered the call.

"Mrs Gaitland." Ginny smiled. "What a pleasant—"

"Ginny, honey, I don't have much time. Can you come outside for a spell so we can talk?"

Ginny nodded and stepped onto the porch, closing the door behind her.

"Am I interrupting your chores or anything? Will your mother be missing your presence?"

"Nope, Ma's gone to Mr McElroy's. What's wrong, you seem—"

"Seem? I am."

Beatrice led Ginny over to a porch swing and they sat down.

"Ginny, what I'm about to tell you—you mustn't utter a single word to another soul."

Her young friend's brown eyes widened.

"Can I trust you?"

Ginny nodded. "Cross m' heart. What is it, Mrs Gaitland?"

Beatrice took a deep breath and spilled everything about the situation—everything, that is, but the brothel visit and her other intimate encounters with Luke.

"Of course I'll accompany you durin' the day. Whatever thing I can help you with, Mrs Gaitland." When Ginny opened her arms to offer Beatrice a hug, Beatrice nearly lost control of her emotions. She'd had no other female to share her feelings with, no familiars whose shoulders she could cry on. These were the times she desperately missed having her mother and sisters near.

"Oh, Ginny, thank you so much," she whispered, not trusting her full voice.

Ginny pulled away and looked into Beatrice's eyes. "We're for the jail then?"

Beatrice sniffed daintily. "My dear, I'll not make you come inside with me, only to the door."

With a faraway look in her eye, Ginny whispered, "I've never seen the inside of a jail before."

"You, Miss Clark, are far too adventurous for your own good." Beatrice sniffed again.

The young girl giggled. "You sound like my pa."

"Listening to your pa would benefit you greatly."

Ginny pulled a face at her, but Beatrice knew she'd have to put her foot down with Ginny once they'd arrived at the jail.

* * * *

Ginny made to step through the front doorway of the marshal's office but Beatrice placed a hand on her friend's arm, stopping her. "Ginny Clark, what do you think you are doing?"

"Come on, Mrs Gaitland, let me just take a peek inside?"

"Ginny, if your mother knew —"

"She'll never know. I won't tell her and neither will you." With that, Ginny strode, bolder than brass, through the marshal's office straight through to the jail room where the prisoners were held.

Luke glanced up then stood. "Well, howdy, Miss Ginny. I'd have never guessed you'd be one of my visitors."

Ginny was sure her cheeks went red. "I came with Mrs Gaitland."

"Well, that was mighty nice of you. I am, however, shocked that she allowed you inside where the animals are kept."

Giggling, Ginny set down the pillow she'd carried for Mrs Gaitland on a nearby chair and smoothed out the front of her cream and peach calico dress. "She didn't allow me nothin'. I came in because I wanted to."

"And why is that, Miss Ginny?" Luke grinned, "You itchin' to find yourself a rugged outlaw and make him your boyfriend?"

"You're a terribly naughty flirt, Luke, you know that?"

Luke folded his arms across his chest. "You think so?" He tipped his head.

Marshal White stood, craning his neck to see where Ginny had gone, then addressed Beatrice, "I trust everything is all right with you, Mrs Gaitland?"

She smiled, set her basket down and handed the used duster to the marshal. "It is, if I could get my escort not to be so curious."

"I'm glad she wasn't here about an hour ago. We had a couple of them cowboys in here, but not for long. When you have friends in high places like Sheriff Behan, you have nothing to worry about." He then returned the duster to its place on a peg in the wall.

"That reminds me, Marshal. I am of a firm belief my fiancé will be found innocent."

His brows shot up and a pleasant smile blossomed on his bearded face. "Your fiancé? You don't say?"

"Mm-hmm." She nodded at his smile, no longer giving a fig what people thought of her abandoning her mourning, and continued.

"I have to confess" — he smiled cordially at her — " — "Mrs White and I thought you too young and pretty to have to endure an entire mourning period. I know it's against decades of decorum, but we thought so just the same."

The marshal's face had gone red. Beatrice supposed he and his wife were the sweetest people in the territory. "How very kind of you, Marshal." She smiled with sincerity.

"Now, my dear, how can I help?"

"You see, Doc Holliday was at the scene of the murder Luke has been accused of and there is a very good possibility he'll oblige Luke and stand as a witness at the trial."

Beatrice watched as the marshal's smile faded. "Oh, Mrs Gaitland. I fear Doc Holliday is not a very good reference for Luke."

"I keep hearing that, Marshal White. However, if he was there — if he was the only one — "

The marshal held up a hand. His face showed a subtle apology for his interrupting her and he shook his head. "I suspect you'll have to start praying for a miracle, my dear."

Beatrice felt her breath leave her lungs, but, before an impending string of tears could be unleashed, she murmured her thanks, picked up her basket and headed for where Luke was being held. Just inside the door, she witnessed a very odd conversation, which tumbled her scattered emotions in yet another direction.

Ginny tilted her head. "I do think you are. And, if it wasn't for Mrs Gaitland, I'd kiss you."

"Well, Ginny, if it wasn't for Mrs Gaitland, and if you were ten years older, I might let you."

"You may think I'm a little girl, but I ain't. Why, I'll be fifteen in just a few weeks."

"Now listen, young lady, I have a kid brother your age — so, the way I see it, you are a little girl."

The intake of Ginny's breath echoed in the room. She stepped forward. "Does he look like *you*?"

Beatrice felt she'd better put a stop to Ginny and her overly forward questions. "What on earth are you two talking about?" She set the basket down then stood with her arms akimbo.

"Ah, there is my sweet Mrs Gaitland. Come over here and let these aching eyes take a look at you."

Beatrice raised an eyebrow in warning and angled her head in a silent gesture to end Luke's presumptuous banter. "Not until I get Ginny out of here. Come on." She guided Ginny from the back room and through the office.

"Good lord, Mrs Gaitland, you have yourself a wicked man there," the young girl whispered.

"Someone needs to teach you that things of that nature aren't said aloud. Now just you never mind about Luke — we'll discuss your behaviour later. And pray your mother doesn't find out where you've been." she softened her stern look then. "Thank you for being my companion. I shouldn't have asked you, but I have no one else." She was truly sincere and hoped that Ginny found her so.

Ginny enveloped Beatrice in a tight embrace. "I'm honoured you asked me, Mrs Gaitland. Come git me when you're in need again."

They said their goodbyes and Ginny left for home.

Beatrice was crossing the office when Marshal White let her know Luke was now under his personal protection, and he'd be taking over the night shifts until after the trial.

"So you won't mind if I linger here during your shift, and provide meals for the prisoner?"

Marshal White dipped his head slightly. "It's a bit unorthodox, but I know and trust you, Mrs Gaitland. Honestly, you'd be saving me from kitchen duty." He smiled.

"Thank you, Marshal, we are indebted to you."

Luke stood when she entered. "Are we all alone, now?" he purred.

"Easy now, tiger. There is a level of dignity to be had, even in a jail." She bent to unload her basket.

He chuckled. "Who says?" From out of the corner of her eye she saw him walk over to the cell door and place his booted foot upon the bottom rung.

Glancing up she asked, "You hungry?"

"More or less. Why don't you close the door and ask me your question again?"

"I'm intrigued." She reached over and quietly shut the door. She turned and saw a sensual smile settle on his lips. A thrill shot up her spine. Ginny was right. He was a wicked, wicked man.

"Care to join your future husband?" With his foot he pushed the door to his cell wide open.

Her lungs flooded with air in surprise. "Does the Marshal know about that door?"

"Yes." Luke shrugged. "He also knows that I know that I'm safer in here than I would be outside." He turned serious. "Now come over here," he demanded gently.

Her limbs tingled with anticipation. Willing her legs to move, she stepped over to Luke. He took her in his arms and joined his lips to hers for a stirring kiss.

When he pulled away just enough to look into her eyes, she skittered her tongue across her lips. "Why do you taste like you've imbibed?"

"I won a full flask of whisky from a cowboy a little while ago."

His warm breath smelt as good as he tasted. "Where is it?" she inhaled, enjoying the scent of him.

"In my bunk. Care to inspect it?"

She grinned. "The flask or your bunk?"

Luke took a deep breath. "Both, if you wish it, Peaches. All that I have is at your disposal, my dear."

"Luke, we shouldn't be fooling about like this. Aren't you hungry?"

"My, my, Mrs Gaitland, aren't we full of questions? And at such a sensitive time."

"Sensitive?"

"Yes, I should be making love to you right now."

She tried to remove herself from his arms, shaking her head adamantly. "We cannot make love in here."

Luke wouldn't let her go. "Why ever not? We've made love in a cave, we've made love in a brothel — why not a jail?"

She fully pulled out of his arms. "Because, just on the other side of that very thin wall yonder sits a lawman, and I'm sure he's not inclined to offer up his back room as a den of iniquities."

Luke smiled — that terribly confident smile at which he was so adept. "And what else?"

"What else, what?"

"What else are you afraid of?"

Beatrice licked her lips again and looked away for a moment. After a brief pause she surrendered her thought. "I'm loud, if you must know." Her cheeks heated.

Luke placed his hand over his heart. "On my honour, madam, you'll never hear a complaint from me." He winked. "I'm curious, though. Did you notice this recently or have you known all along?"

She would have laughed—however, her embarrassment wouldn't allow it. "Now cease your teasing. In the cave or the brothel it didn't matter, but my friend is in the next room!"

"I must confess, I love the fact that you're so free with me you are able to narrate your passion at the top of your lungs."

"That will be enough, *sir*," she warned.

"Now, with *that* I happen to disagree. I'll never get enough of *you*." He hugged her so fiercely she lost her breath.

He released her then retrieved the basket she'd brought in. He placed it upon his cot and sat down, offering her a seat next to it with a pat of his hand.

She obliged and sat down.

Luke pulled out the flask and unscrewed the stopper. "Perhaps if you had a few sips of spirit you'd be less concerned about your," he searched for the right word, "vocalisations."

"Not likely." She watched with rapt attention as he took a long draw.

"What's in there, again?" She indicated the good-sized silver flask with a jerk of her chin.

"Whisky. Good whisky. I'll tell you one thing, that Ringo has taste."

She only intended on grinning but she felt the action to her toes. She darted her gaze to his lips then back to his eyes.

"What?" He slid her a suspicious look.

She debated whether or not to verbalise the thought that begged to be revealed. But, with her very next heartbeat, either good judgement lost out or she gave up on the argument—one or the other had overcome her, and she didn't care which. "I was just wondering what your mouth tastes like," she murmured, curious as a cat crouched at the entrance to a field mouse's den.

At once he corked the flask and tossed the basket of food to the floor—which miraculously landed right side up. Slowly, he eased her to a reclining position on the cot and gave her a deep drink.

Chapter Fifteen

The way in which he was kissing her made her head spin. He tasted so amazingly good that she could have fed off one kiss, needing no further sustenance for the rest of the evening and into the night. His tongue was smooth as it played over hers. His lips were soft and pliant as he guided the kiss, intensifying it one minute then melting into an undemanding bearing—making her think he was relaxing and about to stop, only to build it up again. She hadn't even noticed his hands were under her skirts, sliding up her thighs until his thumbs grazed her nether lips through her bloomers. She squeaked in protest against his mouth. "No!"

"Yes." His fingers surged harder against her.

"No!" She insisted more forcefully and jumped up and away from the cot, crossing her arms over her chest in a resolute manner.

Just then, the marshal opened the door and poked his head in. "There is some sort of ruckus at the Crystal Palace. I'm going to have to lock the doors while I go investigate."

"I understand, Marshal," Beatrice nodded, proud that her voice hadn't betrayed the fact that she'd just had Luke's hands up her skirts, and stepped out of the cell. Although she was pretty sure her cheeks reflected the heat she felt, she pushed the thought to the back of her mind.

"You'll be all right, Mrs Gaitland?"

"Of course I will." She smiled, after which he applied the key to the cell door's lock. She listened as the middle door clicked closed. The keys were hung on the peg and, after a moment, the front door closed.

The moment the bolt slid home, she turned to Luke and the hair on the back of her neck stood on end. He was in the process of unscrewing the flask and, at the same time, was closing in on her like a panther.

He stopped when he could go no further and took a sip of the whisky.

Visually following his actions, she swallowed at the same time he did.

"Care for a drink, my little jailbird?"

Her breath hitched in her chest, making her dizzy with anticipation. She was all too familiar with the rumbling sound his voice made when he was about to make love to her. She nodded and he offered her the flask, holding it up to her lips. After she took a quick sip — which all but scalded her throat — he replaced the lid and flung it onto the cot behind him.

Beatrice opened the door to the office and plucked the keys from the wall. Good lord, she could get into a heap of trouble if the marshal found out what she was about to do. Tossing caution to the four winds, she shut the door and unlocked Luke's cell, leaving the keys dangling in the iron lock. She felt powerful, lusty and perfectly naughty.

Luke moved towards her, swallowing her with his presence. He gathered her in his arms and kissed her silly.

However, this newfound power must have gone to her head. She broke off the kiss and placed a hand on his chest. "Just a moment."

"We only have but a moment, my dear." Luke ignored her hand and flattened his body against hers.

"If anyone knows that, it is I. Let me take the reins," she purred.

Luke raised his eyebrows as he drew back to look her in the eye. "How do you mean?"

She grinned at him. "You are my prisoner now." She heard the authority in her voice and felt it reverberate through her body. She meant to dominate him, positive that the burning trail of whisky helped as it made its way to her belly. She wondered if he would allow this, but there was only one way to find out.

With both hands against his chest, she manoeuvred him so that his back pressed against his iron prison. She took each of his hands and curled his fingers around the bars next to his shoulders. She then smoothed her hands over the soft cotton shirt that covered his muscled torso, and down over the cut planes of his abdomen. The fabric seemed to heat up as she touched him.

"I'm not sure I can let you do what I think you're going to do."

She shushed him. "You don't have a choice," she murmured as she began unbuttoning his fly. Without warning, she knelt before him.

Following a sharp intake of breath, he whispered a warning. "I'll go mad if you—" His sentence didn't finish, but ended in a moan.

She opened her mouth to accommodate his magnificent penis. She felt his warm, velvety-soft length pass over her lips and hoped with all her heart she was doing it right.

She explored him with her tongue, enjoying the unrestrained sounds and cursing coming from her lover—they encouraged her and made her want to pleasure him more. When she began to suck on him, he went silent. Knowing his episode would happen soon, she willingly anticipated the taste of it.

He spoke from above her, panting harshly. "You'd better stop now, Peaches. Your mouth is doing things to me—Oh, God, you'd better stop."

Suddenly he disengaged himself from her and helped her to stand.

"But, Luke—"

Luke turned her so that *her* back was against the bars. He took up one of her hands and kissed her fingertips. "I promise you, when we have all night to ourselves"—he placed the palms of her hands around the bars of their cage just as she had done for him—"you can do that for as long as you like." He finished in a whisper then dropped to his knees in front of her.

She held tight to the bars, barely able to stand as Luke fished through her skirts. Then, all at once, she felt the soft fabric of her bloomers slide over her bottom and down her legs. Her shoes came next.

Luke then pulled her skirts up and behind her, shoving each side through the bars. She was bare from the hips down. Her heart slammed against her ribs. She'd die if she were caught in this wholly scandalous position.

He stood and pressed his body to hers, sliding his fingers between her legs. "But, for now, I must have you like this."

He stroked her with expert hands, playing with the bit of flesh between her legs as he nipped at her neck and ears. She could feel herself swelling as his fingers surrounded her, pulling at her as if he were milking her tiny nubbin. Her episode came hard and fast—but, oh, so exquisitely. Luke covered her mouth with his, absorbing her cries.

Then she felt him enter her, slamming her against the bars at her back. His powerful thrusts urged her convulsions around his manhood, reigniting the tremors. His strength made her want to surrender her very soul to him. She buried her face in his shirt front in the hopes that her passionate cries would be muffled.

Not long after he'd shuddered against her, he murmured in her ear, "I can't wait until I have all night long to be with you."

Unwilling to spoil the moment—and breathless besides—she merely nodded in agreement.

He refastened his fly and helped her with her drawers and shoes. She had just enough time to lock the cell and replace the keys before the marshal's return. Beatrice hoped the keys wouldn't be swinging on their peg when he entered.

After Marshal White unlocked the cell, Luke and Beatrice partook of the delightful picnic lunch from her basket.

"I'm afraid this will be the last my kitchen can provide." She indicated to the fare before them. "I'm positive Allen will be cutting off my allowance after what I've done," she murmured then bit into an apple.

Luke chased a bite of bread down with a swig from his flask. "By that, you mean falling in love with someone else besides him?"

A grim grin briefly passed over her lips and she swallowed. "Call it what you will, but, yes, that's my theory."

Luke raised the cuff of his pant leg and peeled back the top of his boot. He then pulled out two silver dollars from underneath the leather lining and tossed them to Beatrice. "I have a stack of these left. If you will be supplying me with sustenance, it's only right I pay for it. And yours as well."

She smiled, thinking him the most generous man on earth. "Tell you what, I'll go right now and fetch you some sarsaparilla. I'll not have you drunk at all hours of the day from that stuff." She indicated the flask with a tilt of her head.

Luke recapped the fancy decanter and hugged it, making Beatrice giggle and throw her napkin at him.

* * * *

Later that afternoon, well before sundown, Beatrice had visited Nellie Cashmen's restaurant and returned with a hot meal. The marshal paid for a plate for himself, and had asked her to pick up a copy of the latest edition of the *Tombstone Epitaph* as well.

After giving the marshal his meal, she entered the jail to set out her and Luke's supper.

"The strangest thing happened over at the *Epitaph*, Luke," she began as he cut into his steak.

Luke took a bite and he raised his brows in an invitation for her to continue her story.

"Mr Clum, the owner, greeted me strangely when I went to pick up a copy of the paper for Marshal White."

"Did he?" Luke dug into the mashed potatoes.

She bit into a biscuit and nodded.

Luke opened a bottle of sarsaparilla and handed it to her. "Go on," he urged after she'd swallowed.

"Well, first he looked at me as if he'd never seen me before, then he went about bobbing his head as if I were the Queen of England."

Luke considered the situation for a moment. "Perhaps he was merely being polite."

"Perhaps. Then he handed me a stack of the latest issue of the *Epitaph*. I told him I only wanted one for Marshal White, but he insisted I take one for myself as well. He suggested I read the supplement page, furnished by a freelance writer here in town—a Mrs Sanderson."

"That is peculiar. Where's the paper?"

Beatrice retrieved it from next to her reticule and handed it to Luke, who opened it and began to peruse the headlines of the insert page.

"Aw, hell," he muttered. "Listen to this—'*Celebrity In Our Midst or Bird In Our Cage? It has come to our attention that one Lucas Hughson, who has been residing in and around our humble camp for at least two weeks, is connected to the Hughsons of Virginia, close friends with the extremely wealthy Vanderbilt family—the royalty of America. However, it's not all roses for our young Lucas. In the last few days, Lucas Hughson's face has appeared on a handful of wanted posters for the murder of a Mr Cramdon Davis, formerly of Bellevue, Nebraska. But we'd be keeping information from you if we didn't tell you the best part. It seems the widow to the late pastor, Lindley Gaitland, has taken a shine to young Luke. Upon further investigation, we found out Mrs Gaitland's given name is Beatrice Victoria King, whose family also boasts of a social connection with the Vanderbilts. The trial will be set soon. Keep reading* The Society Page *for more on this intriguing story. With her eye on Tombstone Society, Mrs M. Sanderson.*"

By the time Luke finished the article, Beatrice could barely breathe. "Good heavens," she gasped. "This story is going to spread all the way to New York and back. Did she have to be so...so *sensational* about it?"

"I can't even imagine the ramifications that will occur if my father gets a hold of these people," Luke murmured, shaking his head.

She swallowed and it practically echoed off the walls. "Will he be very angry at you? Will you be in trouble?"

"Sweetheart, *the world* will be in trouble when he finds out. We're Irish, if that lends any sort of explanation — and he has a reputation for defending his family like a mother bear protects her cubs. Trust me. I've seen it first-hand."

Trying to observe things from a positive perspective, Beatrice attempted a smile. "Well, perhaps he won't find out. What if he's abroad or something?"

"Abroad or not, my father is so well connected I often wonder why they didn't name the telephone after him."

Beatrice looked down at her food, her appetite gone.

* * * *

Just before dawn, Marshal White announced the end of the double shift he'd taken. Beatrice decided she'd go back to the cottage until it was close to the time the marshal would return for work. Luke agreed it would be a good idea to do so, and told her to stay out of sight in the meantime.

"Can I ask you a special favour, Peaches?" Luke asked from his cot as she was preparing to leave.

"Of course, anything."

Luke looked her up and down in a slow, lazy, sensual manner.

She shook her finger at him. "I might amend, only if it is something that can be done in the light of day with all of the windows and doors open."

His wicked grin practically melted her very bones.

"Whatever you are about to say, Mr Hughson, you'd better swallow it up," she warned him in a motherly tone.

"Aw, shucks," he chuckled. "What I was going to ask, until you distracted me so deliciously, was for a razor and some soap." He took his jaw between his fingers and gave it a scratch. "I usually shave every morning and haven't had the opportunity of late. My gear is back at the cave."

"Certainly I will," she smiled at him and thought he looked rather rugged with stubble lightly shadowing his cheeks and chin.

She kissed Luke goodbye and, afterwards, Marshal White escorted her home.

* * * *

With the bundle of necessities for Luke tucked under her arm, Beatrice made her way to Ginny Clark's in the late afternoon. Just as the house came into sight, Allen stepped from a saloon tent.

"Where are you going, Beatrice? Out for another liaison?"

She hurried along. "I do not wish to speak with you, Allen. Leave me alone."

Allen fell into step with her. "You know, Beatrice, you should be more civil to me. I will be your lord and master one day soon."

She let slip from her lips a sob that was part laughter and part fear. "You will be nothing of the kind. Now, I'll ask you once more to leave me alone."

Allen reached for her and pulled on her arm in order to make her stop. "You can save his life, Beatrice."

"How?" she blurted, knowing exactly to whom he was referring.

"Ah, I see I've got your attention now." He took a deep breath through his nose as if he had all the time in the world. "If you marry me and stop seeing him, I won't testify against your paramour."

"You are an ignorant man, Allen Gaitland." She wrenched her arm from his grasp and made to walk away when he spoke again.

"He will be hanged, Beatrice. And you will have no other choice but to marry me. I have control over Lindley's money, for God's sake."

She took a few steps in the direction in which she was headed and spoke to him over her shoulder without meeting his eyes. "I don't care if you have control over the entire camp, I'll never marry you, Allen, so get the thought out of your head."

"Beatrice!" he barked.

But, before he could delay her further, she broke into a run, whispering a prayer of thanks when she saw Ginny's mother in the midst of sweeping her porch. Allen would not follow and pester her with witnesses about.

"Hello, Mrs Clark," she called out.

"Hello, Mrs Gaitland!" Mrs Clark waved then called to Ginny. "Virginia, Mrs Gaitland is here."

"Ma, don't call me that!" Ginny protested from inside the house, clearly irritated.

Mrs Clark smiled and winked at Beatrice. "But that's the name I gave you, darlin'."

"I can't stand that name, and you very well know it!"

Breathing abnormally fast from her short sprint, Beatrice smiled, mostly in relief. She would've sat through a dozen mother-daughter arguments as long as they kept Allen away.

Chapter Sixteen

Of all the things to forget, a mirror for Luke had caused Beatrice the most trouble.

From her reclined position on Luke's cot, she recalled how the situation had got out of hand.

Luke had insisted she shave him, deeming it her punishment for not procuring a way in which to see his own progress. He'd set up a stool and small table in his cell, then placed a bowl of water they'd borrowed from the marshal next to the straight razor and soap mug.

Once Beatrice'd had his face thoroughly soaped, and the frighteningly sharp razor in her hand poised above his cheek, he'd insisted she straddle his lap for the best angle. Regardless of the many protestations about decorum she'd uttered — to which Luke had merely shrugged — she conceded, but had still thought it a terribly brazen thing to do.

Even as she'd dragged the blade slowly down his face, his hands had lifted the front of her skirts. She'd verbalised her objection, but dared not move away, afraid she'd cut him. The moment his fingers had found their mark, she couldn't have moved if she'd wanted to.

Luke had whispered to her that, even if someone had looked into the room of cells, they would have seen only a woman shaving a man.

Beatrice shifted on the cot as she remembered the way he'd so skilfully toyed with her. Not having been given the blessing of completion owing to the marshal being in the next room, she'd finished shaving him and backed away, the front of her skirts coming to rest once again where they belonged, sweeping the floor.

She watched as he blindly inspected her job with the back of his hand.

"You did a fine job, Peaches," he murmured and rose from his seat.

Beatrice dropped her gaze to the bulge behind his fly that demanded her attention and she licked her lips. "*You* didn't." Then her voice fell to a whisper. "I was unable to reach my episode."

Luke grinned wickedly. "Episode. I like that. It's deceptively seductive."

"Well, what else do you call it?"

He pulled her to him and whispered, "An orgasm, for one."

Her entire body lit up, like a burning match set to a dried barn—the word rolled through her in one glorious shudder. He was the one who was deceptively seductive, it certainly wasn't her. He teased her, stroked her and said naughty things to her every chance he got. She'd have been content just shaving him, but he'd started the dough rising, and now nothing could be done about it. Nothing except—

She untangled herself from his arms and went over to pick up the bowl of used water. Without looking up at Luke, she headed for the marshal's office.

"Where are you going with that? I'm not finished."

"Neither am I." She'd shot the statement over her shoulder, hoping he would catch on to the double meaning.

Moments later she and the marshal came into the room and he shut and locked the cell—with her inside.

"Next to McElroy's store, you say?"

"Yes, Marshal. I saw them fill the barrel with fresh water this morning. Thank you so much." She smiled.

"I'll be just a few moments, then," Marshal White said and closed the door between the jail and the office.

She froze as she listened for the lock on the front door. When the bolt sounded, she turned to Luke.

"Peaches! I'm shocked at the misleading distraction you've created for our jailor," Luke taunted, clearly unperturbed and feigning innocence so poorly she could have laughed.

"Tease me about it later. Now give me my orgasm before I go mad," she fairly growled.

They came together in a frenzy, only opening their clothes enough to get the job done.

Shoving her skirts aside and parting the split in her bloomers, he bent her forward and stroked her between the legs as he took her from behind. Beatrice steeled herself using the cell bars, legs spread and hips high, accepting his pounding thrusts and a dozen or so well placed slaps on her bottom, which both surprised her and added fuel to her fire.

Her reward for her little diversion was a spectacular orgasm that left her just about unable to continue standing. Thank God her breathing had returned to normal as the marshal came in with the fresh water.

After thanking the marshal, she returned to the cot. Her gaze landed on Luke, who was carefully drying the shaving items. He took such good care of his things and the people in his circle—the thought that he might not be able to try his hand at his family's plantation caused tears to well up in her eyes.

* * * *

A few days later, Beatrice took Ginny and her mother around to the different merchants in preparation for Stone Soup Hour. The town's folk were as generous as ever—regardless of the *Epitaph's* attempt at scandal. Mrs Clark was particularly happy about acquiring the leftovers.

Once the fire was roaring, the benches arranged, and the stew bubbling away while Ginny stirred, Beatrice felt she could retire from the scene.

"I'll be off now, ladies. Thank you again, Mrs Clark. I'm sure the miners will be most appreciative of your adoption of Stone Soup Hour." She smiled, relieved the Clark's had volunteered to continue the ministry. The sun dipped below the horizon of hills to the west and the miners had been arriving steadily for the past half-hour or so.

Beatrice was about to bid her good evenings to Ginny and her mother when Allen hailed them.

"Well, this is a cosy sight," he said, his voice glib and unflustered.

She felt the urge to drop the dishrag she was holding and flee. Instead, she took a fortifying breath and squared her shoulders. To all the world, Allen was a mild-mannered citizen, but very recently she had become acquainted with a different side of him. He was as greedy and demanding as any dastardly outlaw could be. For the hundredth time since he'd invaded her life in Tombstone, Allen reminded her of Lindley in the way he held his faux face up like a Mardi Gras mask on a stick.

Beatrice noticed that Ginny had stopped stirring and was standing like a statue, holding fast to the handle of the spoon, staring down into the pot. She took a few steps over to Ginny and placed a hand on her shoulder while Allen and Mrs Clark exchanged pleasantries.

"I didn't tell Ma anything about Pastor Allen. She still thinks highly of him," Ginny whispered.

"Good. Let her. I'd not wish to be the cause of any bad blood between them. His colours will show through eventually anyway, you'll see." She glanced Allen's way then turned back to Ginny. "It'll be all right—now don't be afraid."

Ginny responded with a slight nod and began stirring the contents of the cauldron once again.

"Beatrice," Allen addressed her from next to Mrs Clark in an amiable manner, and continued when she spun to face him. "I'm so glad you are here. I would love to join you for a bowl of soup. I'm fairly starving." He ended with a grin that didn't reach his eyes.

Sure you are, she silently sneered, *probably because you've had no one to cook for you recently.* Previously, he'd been so repulsed by the thought of dining on the soup that it was obvious he was up to something. Did he think she was so stupid that she wouldn't notice his sudden change of heart? Sweeping off her hands to cover a shudder of revulsion, she answered him as sweet as pie. "I'm sorry, Pastor, but I have plans for supper elsewhere." She watched a flash of anger pass over his features then turned back to Ginny, but her young friend had fled the scene. Beatrice scanned the area, her heart suddenly doing double-time. There was one thing she didn't want, and that was to be alone with Allen.

"Well then, allow me to escort you to your next destination."

"No, that won't be necessary. Besides, you said you are starving and I'd not wish to put you out."

"Not at all. In fact, I'm happy to do it." He grinned, but Beatrice saw nothing but a devil.

"Oh, Mrs Gaitland!" Ginny called out from the opening of the tent. "These gentlemen are ready to take you into town now."

Two very large miners appeared behind Ginny, making her look like a toddler in the presence of adults.

Nodding, Beatrice acknowledged both men then winked at Ginny. "Wonderful. Let us withdraw, gentlemen." Without sparing Allen even a civil glance, Beatrice thanked Mrs Clark again, then she and the men departed.

* * * *

Beatrice was sure the miners who had escorted her to town were angels in disguise. *What on earth had Ginny said to them?* They'd walked on either side of her like sentries, and doffed their hats to her once she was secure inside Marshal White's office, offering any other assistance within their power.

Luke had been pacing like a tiger in a cage when she'd finally entered the jail. When he saw her come in he nearly bowled her over, throwing his arms around her. "Where have you been? I was beside myself with worry." Not allowing her to answer, he kissed her lips and face as if to reassure himself of her presence.

"I am safe, but you are very intuitive — Allen did try to stir up trouble. However, it seems the heavenly realm is on my side tonight." Beatrice told Luke the story while he held her close.

"Thank God. I was hoping I wouldn't have to bust through the marshal's office and go looking for you."

Tears stung Beatrice's eyes. "Luke," she whispered, her emotions squeezing the sound to almost nothing. "You always make me feel so cherished and cared for."

He took her by the face and covered her cheeks with kisses. "I love you, Peaches." His breath stirred the hair at her temple. "I'll protect you with my life, forever. You can count on it."

"I'm the luckiest woman in the world."

"Yes, let's hope your luck holds out, sweetheart."

She knew of what Luke spoke, and prayed to God it would.

* * * *

The day of the trial arrived and the route to their destination was laborious both physically and internally for Beatrice. It annoyed her terribly that, because the crime had happened outside of the Arizona territory, the town's courthouse wouldn't suffice for this trial. So she endured the long, hot road to Benson.

Apprehensive about the sensation she and Luke had caused, Beatrice had avoided any news from the outside world, including the *Epitaph*, for the last three weeks.

Although Luke had reassured her that all would work itself out, she knew in her heart that things were bleak at best. She'd not heard from Doc Holliday, even though she had written three notes to him and Kate, slipping them under the door of their room at Fly's herself.

The butterflies in her stomach were weighty and wet, like the heavy raindrops that had pelted the jail's roof the night before.

Beatrice rode in a coach with Marshal White behind the wagon that carried Luke. All she could do the whole way to the courthouse was lean out of the side window and stare at the prison wagon ahead of them, which carried the love of her life. No matter how hard she tried, she was unable to see him through the tiny barred window at the top of the door. They must have shackled him to the bench on the inside, making it impossible to stand or even crouch to see out of the only window.

When they arrived at the courthouse, it looked as if the inhabitants of Benson were awaiting a parade. The streets were lined with people hoping for a show. With a heavy heart, she watched as two deputies led Luke inside. She and Marshal White followed shortly after.

Thankfully, the marshal found them a seat up front, right behind Luke and the lawyer assigned to his case. She wanted so badly to hold Luke's hand. However, his shackles remained locked around his wrists as if he might escape the first chance he got. They both knew that, if he tried to run, the mob would lynch him for sure. She couldn't help but think that Allen had had something to do with Luke's chains.

Allen sat across the way, next to the prosecuting lawyer, where he made sure that the attorney's glass was filled to the brim with water, and that the table before him was free of dust and other non-existent debris. Beatrice looked away as her nerves would not allow her gaze to lock with his, not even for a second.

When Judge Wells Spicer took the bench, Beatrice found herself unable to follow the legal jargon. Her ears only stayed open to hear one of two phrases — 'Guilty' or 'Not guilty'. She hoped with all her heart for the latter.

It warmed Beatrice's heart when Doc Holliday took the stand in defence of Luke. She looked around for Kate, but she was nowhere to be seen.

Doc was a very well-spoken man, and Beatrice found his testimony appealing — until he was cross-examined by the prosecution.

"John Henry Holliday, you are familiar with knife fights over silly little trifles such as a game of cards, are you not?"

Doc didn't answer. He glared at the mousey lawyer from his seat on the witness stand as a stone settled in Beatrice's stomach. This was exactly what Doc had wanted to avoid.

The lawyer glanced at the jury. "Dr Holliday's silence may be taken as consent."

"And your question, sir, is only trying to defame my character —" Doc began in his gravelly voice.

Not a second later, Judge Spicer's gavel put an end to his interruption. "I will have order in my courtroom," he commanded and set the wooden hammer down.

The defence lawyer assigned to Luke came out of his seat. "I'll have to object to this line of questioning, Your Honour. Dr Holliday is not on trial here and the enquiry has nothing to do with this case."

Judge Spicer considered the attorney's motion. "Sustained. Would the prosecution please retract and restate the question, possibly in a more suitable way — and stick to the matter at hand."

The prosecuting lawyer looked at Holliday, smirked, then returned his gaze to the judge. "I withdraw the question, Your Honour, and have nothing further to ask."

As Beatrice shifted in her seat in order not to double over in despair, Marshal White patted her hand in sympathy — or was it encouragement? She couldn't tell. Recalling how he'd warned her that Doc's deposition might be disregarded by his peers, her heart felt as if it were plummeting to her feet.

The judge dismissed Doc from the witness stand. As he passed them, Doc nodded his farewell to Luke then Beatrice, and left the courtroom without looking back.

The testimonies that followed were mere character references for Luke. Her heart overflowed, thankful for each one. Mr McElroy told how Luke had been a dependable, hard worker while under his employ, and Marshal White told the court he'd had no trouble whatsoever while Luke was in his care.

When Marshal White stepped down from the witness stand, Beatrice glanced around the courtroom in awe of how many of the townsfolk had turned out in support of Luke. She ignored the strangers who had clearly attended seeking sensation.

Beatrice deemed the judge gracious for allowing the citizens of Tombstone to speak, but the prosecuting lawyer demanded that their testimonies be dismissed as they were not witness to the actual event.

When the time came for the prosecution to call its first witness, Allen strutted over to take the stand. He smiled first at the jury, then at Judge Spicer as if they were all old friends and Allen had been living amongst them all his life. Beatrice's stomach nearly turned over. Allen was doing everything possible to sway anyone with any say in this trial over to his side. *As if he could,* Beatrice harrumphed, trying to convince herself.

"My dear friends and neighbours," he addressed the jury. "It is very possible you will discount what I have to say as well as you did the others, but I must do my duty before God and the citizens of this territory, and tell you what has been going on in your own back yards."

So sayeth the phony pastor. Beatrice couldn't even look at the bastard. She stared at Luke's shoulders, against which she longed to press herself and plug her ears.

Allen indicated Luke. "This evader of the law, who has been on the run ever since the incident in Bellevue, Nebraska, has been hiding out in the Dragoon Mountains. Now, I ask you, if you were innocent of a crime, would you need to hide?"

Beatrice's eyes watered. Allen's was the same argument she'd had for her ex-husband when he'd brought that pink whore to their cottage. She found herself unable to breathe and made ready to bolt, but Marshal White must have felt her distress. His hand came to rest on hers as it gripped the bench on which they sat.

The courtroom had stirred at Allen's last statement, and again the judge used his gavel to quiet down those in attendance.

"Pastor Gaitland," Judge Spicer began, "we truly appreciate your testimony. However, just like the other men the prosecuting attorney dismissed, neither were you a witness to the actual event." The judge shot an authoritative look to the attorney at the table in front of Allen. "Had the others counted for something in his eyes, I would allow your testimony to stand along with theirs. However—"

"I understand completely," Allen said, raising his hand in a friendly gesture of surrender. Not a moment later, the judge dismissed him from the stand.

It was obvious to Beatrice that he'd wanted only to make his view known to the jury, the dirty, low-down varmint. She hoped he tripped on his way back to his seat.

Beatrice felt Allen's eyes on her as he returned to his chair. Powerless to control the action, she glanced up at him. He was smiling. Slyly, he tugged at his collar in a dramatic fashion with his index finger, his eyes widening briefly in emphasis.

As fast as possible, she transferred her gaze to the floor in front of her. She'd heard loud and clear what he was conveying without words.

The jury was dismissed to make their decision and Marshal White offered to take Beatrice outside. "Come, dear, you need some fresh air. You look as pale as a ghost."

"No, thank you, Marshal. It is my deepest wish to remain with Luke," she refused and retracted her elbow from his light grasp.

Nodding, the marshal quit the room and she leant forward over the low barrier that separated Luke from her. She longed to throw herself into his arms, but knew most of the attendees in the courtroom had hung on her every movement that morning, and she was loath to give their frenzy any more fuel.

"Luke," she whispered brokenly.

He tipped his chair back. "Hello, Peaches," he murmured, smooth and quiet so only she could hear.

The back of his head was mere inches from her face. Her barely functioning senses took in his scent and she nearly sobbed. "How can you be so calm? I can scarce draw breath."

His ample shoulders rose slightly then came to rest in a relaxed manner. "It's over, sweetheart. I told you there was nothing we could have done."

"Don't think that way," she sobbed and gripped the bannister. "You mustn't even say it aloud."

Luke turned his head and looked at her tenderly, caressing her face with his gaze. "Sweetheart, I want you to know I'm grateful for having been allowed the time with you."

She strained to get as close to him as possible. "You make it sound as if the decision has already been made." Her tears overflowed then, but she ignored the wet trails on her cheeks.

"It has, my love. I can feel it," he murmured and turned so that he was facing the front of the courtroom.

His nonchalant attitude caused panic to well up inside her. "No, I won't allow it. I won't lose you!" She could barely get the words out of her closing throat.

She hadn't noticed that Marshal White had settled himself next to her again until the jurors were taking their seats in the box. She started at how quickly they'd returned, and noticed they were looking far too sombre for the outcome to be positive. She wept silently but kept her eyes on Luke, as if memorising his very essence.

When Marshal White placed a hand on her shoulder she glanced back at him. He shook his head in sympathy then signalled her to sit back. Just before she did, Luke turned to her. "Peaches, whatever happens, I love you."

Trying desperately to muffle her sobs, Beatrice was physically incapable of returning Luke's sentiment as the marshal guided her back against the bench and handed her a clean handkerchief.

Settling the courtroom with his gavel, Judge Spicer turned to the jury. "Have you reached a verdict?"

The juror on the end stood. "Yes, Your Honour, we have."

Doubling over, unable to inhale enough air to sustain her, Beatrice reached out to the railing for support as the jury was about to end the life of her beloved.

"Stop the proceedings! Stop, I say!" a voice bellowed from the entrance at the rear of the courtroom.

Chapter Seventeen

A collective inhalation was heard all around and, with wide eyes, Beatrice turned along with everyone else to see who would have the audacity to interrupt the proceedings in such a demanding way.

Three men, one tall with wide shoulders, all of them neatly dressed and with a male juvenile in tow, came bounding down the centre aisle. The boy seeped into the crowd at the command of the tall one, and the three men continued to the bench where Judge Spicer sat.

"Wells, you'd best take a recess and hear these men out." An impeccably dressed man in an expensive-looking grey suit indicated the newcomers with whom he'd just entered.

"What's this all about, John?" Judge Spicer shook his head as if to convey that the suggestion was going to be denied. "The jury has already reached a verdict in this case."

The shortest of the three men spoke then. "And it doesn't look like a positive one." He indicated with a nod of his head to the juror box.

"Damn it, Wendell!" the tall one bellowed at the man who had commented on the jury. "I swear I'll buy this town, this county, and every territory and scrap of dried-up land from here to the Pacific if I have to!"

"Uh..." Wendell cleared his throat. "My name is Jonas Wendell, Your Honour. I am — "

"I know who you are." Judge Spicer's eyes went wide. "You're Cornelius Vanderbilt's attorney."

After the courtroom had settled down after another hit of Judge Spicer's gavel, Mr Wendell smiled. "I'm flattered you recognise my name, Your Honour."

"What is this all about, Mr Wendell?"

The man Judge Spicer had first spoken to interrupted. "Wells, if you know what's good for you, you'll hear these men out. Mr Hughson is dead serious about changing Pima County into Hughson County. And I'll wager neither of us will get re-elected if the voters lose their jobs in the aftermath."

Hughson? For the umpteenth time that day Beatrice felt her breath leave her.

"You all right, Mrs Gaitland?" Marshal White whispered.

She swallowed and answered with a nod — the only action she could muster.

One of the jurors, a little man with thick glasses and a plaid bow tie, raised his hand.

Judge Spicer noticed and turned to the box. "Yes, Mr Wilcox?"

The man cleared his throat and stood. "Judge, I — I'd like to change my vote."

Judge Spicer nodded and after a moment issued an invitation. "Does anyone else on the jury care to revisit the evidence?"

There was a stirring in the juror box as the men briefly turned to make eye contact with each other. One of the men raised his hand, then two more joined in, followed by the rest.

While the jurors filed out of the room, Beatrice felt things were about to take a turn for the better. She dabbed at her eyes with the handkerchief and leant over to Marshal White. "Who is the man in the grey suit?"

"John Frémont, Arizona's territorial governor."

Had Beatrice not been sitting down, she'd probably have fallen over.

Luke turned his head and smiled at Beatrice, who then whispered to him while ignoring the murmurings in the courtroom. "Your comment about your father being well connected was a terrible understatement."

"Indeed." He smirked. "Had Mr Wendell and Governor Frémont not been available, I'm sure he would have stormed in here with the Almighty Himself."

Beatrice looked up, her eyes gone wide as Mr Hughson approached his son.

Luke turned to face the front as if he'd felt his father's presence draw near the table.

"Making yourself laugh, are you, Lucas?" His father's Irish brogue was quite pronounced. "We'll speak on this later."

"Certainly, Father, provided there is a later, unless you meant the hereafter."

"Luke!" Beatrice reprimanded.

Mr Hughson's gaze shifted from his son then softened when it landed on her. "And whom do we have here?"

Good heavens. Is this great bear of a man being flirtatious?

Luke cleared his throat. "You're not going to believe this one," he murmured.

Mr Hughson glanced at his son. "I'm standing at a murder trial, where my eldest son, while innocent, is about to be named the guilty party. I think I would believe anything right about now."

Luke conceded with a nod. "Father," he indicated Beatrice with shackled hands, "this is Mrs Beatrice Gaitland. However, you may remember her as Beatrice Victoria King."

Mr Hughson's lips parted, if only for a moment, then he reached out for her hand. When she offered it, he placed a kiss across her gloved knuckles. "My dear Mrs Gaitland, how you have blossomed." His gaze fairly sparkled.

Having no idea what to say, but feeling the burn in her cheeks, Beatrice merely smiled. She hadn't seen him since she was a very young girl, but she could see now where Luke got his masculine good looks.

Leaning towards his father, Luke murmured, "Get your own filly, Kane."

Beatrice almost giggled when Mr Hughson's eyebrows shot up. Instead, she politely removed her hand from his warm grasp.

The jury re-entered and filed back into the box. Beatrice took her place next to Marshal White and Mr Hughson joined the men at the foot of Spicer's bench.

"Well?" Spicer asked the jurors, sounding beyond annoyed.

Mr Wilcox stood and spoke. "We, the jury, find the defendant not guilty of the murder of Mr Cramdon Davis."

Along with the rest of the room, Beatrice shot to her feet. She raised her face to the ceiling, unsure if she was laughing or crying with relief. Drowned out by the tumult in the courtroom, she thanked God out loud. Exchanging a joyful hug with Marshal White, she then hurriedly made her way around the railing.

Luke, who had shown his gratitude to the lawyer assigned to him with a nod, watched with a dimpled smile as Beatrice flew to him. Lifting his hands, which were still cuffed, he threaded her through his arms and claimed her lips.

She melted into him, not giving a fig who saw. Her senses swimming, she almost missed Mr Hughson bellow for the key to his son's shackles.

As Luke held her, and rocked her, Beatrice embraced him with every ounce of strength left in her body and wept into his shirt.

Luke's father slapped him on the back in congratulation, but he refused to release Beatrice, even after someone unlocked his manacles — and she didn't mind in the least.

"Son, isn't it a bit undignified for Mrs Gaitland to be held so in public?" He'd spoken so that only Luke and Beatrice could have heard him.

"If you had a woman in your arms like Mrs Gaitland, you'd not let her go either."

Sniffing, Beatrice smiled and tilted her head to gauge the look on Mr Hughson's face.

Mr Hughson continued, "Well, isn't Mr Gaitland going to have a thing or two to say about all this?"

"Not unless he can contact me about my fiancée from beyond the grave." Luke chuckled and Beatrice choked on her laughter.

"Ah," was all the response his father provided.

A lanky blond-headed adolescent boy emerged from the crowd and stood next to Mr Hughson. Beatrice immediately recognised the family resemblance in his crystal-blue eyes.

"Well, Runt, I'm so glad you could make my party," Luke teased the boy, who was a scant half-foot shorter than him.

"The name is Rory, Ace," he murmured sardonically to Luke then focused on Beatrice. "Please excuse my brother. His years away from society have apparently rendered him mannerless." He bowed slightly at the waist.

Smiling up at Rory, Beatrice giggled. "I remember you, Rory. Although you were too young to recall, I may have changed your nappies."

Rory brought his fist to his chest with a thump. "I've been shot down in my prime, by a beautiful woman," he lamented while his brother laughed mockingly at him.

Shaking her head in a lighthearted apology, Beatrice removed one of her hands and placed it upon Rory's arm. "Fear not, good sir." She grinned. "I'm only teasing. I think you were about nine or so when your family visited ours."

"And still in nappies," Luke taunted.

"I've had just about all I can take from you, Ace," Rory warned.

"Enough, you two," Mr Hughson barked.

Beatrice turned to Mr Hughson. "You can't take the boy out of the man…"

Mr Hughson retrieved Beatrice's hand from Rory's arm. "No, but I bet you could." He made to place a kiss across the backs of her lace-covered fingers, when Luke pulled her away.

"No. Mine."

Laughing, Beatrice turned to Mr Hughson. "Someone's spent far too much time with that ol' Blarney Stone."

Just then, Ginny came running up and addressed Beatrice. "Mrs Gaitland! I wasn't allowed in! I've been outta' my head with worry, and then I heard—" Almost in tears, she stopped her ranting and reached out to hug Beatrice.

Beatrice nudged out of Luke's arms and embraced Ginny. "You are so sweet to have come all this way for us. Is your mother with you?"

Ginny sniffed daintily and nodded. "Yup, she's waitin' outside."

Releasing Ginny, Beatrice handed her a handkerchief and patted her shoulder. "Well I'll just have to thank her too. In the meantime, let me introduce you to Luke's father, Mr Hughson, and Luke's brother, Rory."

Ginny turned and politely shook Mr Hughson's hand, exchanged pleasantries then shifted her gaze to Rory.

Beatrice felt great pride for Ginny. Her young friend's smile had remained steady, even though her eyes betrayed her thoughts.

Rory took Ginny's hand and bowed over it. He then turned to Luke. "Shame on you, Ace, keeping all the pretty girls to yourself."

"Rory, you little snake, could you be more obvious?"

Everyone turned to Beatrice when she cut in. "That from the *king* of obvious?"

Luke's eyes crinkled, but he smothered the grin. "Whose side are you on, sweetheart?"

Chuckling, Beatrice shifted her focus to Mr Hughson, who seemed to be having a grand time watching his sons. "Do they bicker in this fashion often?"

Mr Hughson's grin widened and he nodded. "Ever since Rory grew hair on his —"

"Hey!" Rory protested, interrupting his father. "There are ladies present." He indicated Ginny with a tilt of his head and to Beatrice with raised eyebrows.

"I was going to say chest," Mr Hughson said, with his palms facing the ceiling in mock innocence.

Along with the party who had descended upon the courtroom like avenging angels, Luke and Beatrice joined Mr Hughson for luncheon. In addition, he insisted on treating Mrs Clark and Ginny. They celebrated not only Luke's freedom, but he and Beatrice's engagement.

As far as Allen was aware, no one had witnessed him when he'd retired from the court room following the reading of the verdict—the *second* verdict, to be precise. It was painfully obviously to him that since the justice system was riddled with holes, he'd have to be the one to serve that little bastard and his whore the punishment they deserved

* * * *

"My father's stage leaves tomorrow morning for Tucson. I understand he has a string of private Pullmans to take his party back to the East Coast." Luke nuzzled Beatrice's forehead with his own as they stood on her front porch later that afternoon. "We could go with him..." His voice trailed off, as if he were afraid of her answer.

"So, your offer still stands to make me your wife?"

"Good God, yes!" He picked her up and hugged her so tight she lost her breath, then set her on her feet.

"Then yes, I'll go with you. There isn't anything for me here. I mean, I'll miss the Clarks—Ginny promises to be a beautiful woman. I just wish there was more I could do for her."

Luke chuckled. "You mean beyond keeping her and my brother from pouncing on each other with all their youthful cravings?"

"Well, something like that. There are things she needs to be taught—and a handful of things she needs to be *un*-taught." Sobering, she looked into Luke's eyes. "Where will you go after you leave me here at the house?"

"I need to fetch my personal effects back at the cave. I didn't want to ask you to go—you've had a difficult day."

"Me? You were the one they nearly hanged." He shrugged and she continued. "May I go with you?"

"You sure you want to come? It's a long walk there and back."

"I do. I want to be with you—every moment of every day for the rest of my life."

He smiled down at her. "Excellent. Shall we, then?"

* * * *

The clouds gathered in the sky above as Beatrice and Luke approached the dirt cave.

She gazed into the rapidly greying sky as Luke entered.

"I hope we make it back before the storm hits," Luke said over his shoulder as he took his knapsack in hand.

A loud click—the unmistakable sound of a shotgun cocking—gained their attention. They froze. Allen held a gun, which he'd pointed at Beatrice. The scene was terribly familiar to her and she berated herself for letting her guard down, as if the danger was over. Would the Gaitland brothers ever let her be?

Her breath stalled in her throat as Allen spoke.

"I just couldn't let you win, Hughson."

"Then kill me, Gaitland, but don't harm Beatrice."

"No!" The word had slipped from between Beatrice's lips in a gasp.

Allen laughed. "Don't you worry about Beatrice. I'll want my wife in one piece." He transferred the double-barrel of the gun to point at Luke and walked towards him into the shallow cave. "It's you whom I intend to split in two."

"So put the shotgun down and fight me like a man."

"Oh, I don't think so. Say goodbye to your paramour," Allen said to Beatrice and raised the gun to fire.

As fast as lightning, Luke threw his heavy knapsack and hit Allen in the gut. The gun went off, splintering the only support beam visible from the previous cave-in. The cave collapsed, sending a cloud of dirt towards Beatrice, who could do nothing but scream.

For a few moments she stood, unable to move, until something in the back of her mind, something that had to do with pure survival, told her, in no uncertain terms, *Dig*.

Choking on the dust that filled her throat and doing her best to eject the powdery earth from her lungs, she dived onto the hill of rock and dirt. Clawing at the earth with burning fingers she pushed great handfuls of soil to the side as she yelled for Luke.

"Oh, God, no!" she sputtered. "Please be alive, Luke, you hear me? Luke! Don't you die! Can you hear me, Luke?" Panic took over. "Luke!" She began to cry. "Don't you die!"

She came across Luke's knapsack and pulled the heavy bundle from the rubble. Tossing it aside, she continued to dig and cry, calling to Luke as she did so.

Suddenly, from the other side of the hole she'd created, some dirt fell away and a hand seemed to be digging towards her. When she recognised the shirtsleeve to be Luke's, she sobbed with relief. They worked together to remove enough of the debris for him to be able to push through to the outside.

When he was clear of the cave, she threw her arms around him and sobbed while he shushed her.

"All right, sweetheart. It's all right."

She pulled away to make sure he'd emerged all in one piece. Dust covered him from head to toe and he had a few scratches, but he was —

"Oh, dear God! You're hurt!" she shouted, and gawked at the dirt-caked bloodstain. The stain spanned from his chest to his hip.

"Beatrice, look at me." His undemanding voice calmed her instantly. When her eyes met his, he continued, "It's not my blood, sweetheart. It's Allen's."

With an inhalation of nearly dust-free air, she gazed on the now closed mouth of the cave.

"I'm willing to bet he didn't survive."

She collapsed against Luke. "God, it could have been you in there."

"I know. But it wasn't."

She felt his arms curl around her back.

When she began to cry again, Luke soothed her as best he could with reassuring words.

Pulling away, Luke pointed at something over her shoulder. There she saw how Allen must have got to the cave. A horse stood nibbling on the dry bush that served as a hitching post.

"Come on," he said and took her by the hand, grabbing his knapsack and heading to the horse.

As they began their slow ride back to town, the sky opened up and poured forth warm summer rain. She lifted her face to Heaven, thanking God for Luke's safety, allowing the rain to melt away her stress and, moreover, wash away the pain of her past.

"Finally, the perfect amount of rain," she murmured to the sky.

* * * *

Soaked through to the skin yet none too clean, they arrived at the edge of Beatrice's property. Luke reminded her that this was where they would usually say goodbye.

She smiled and lifted her face so she could look into his eyes. "But not this time."

He hugged her to him and kissed her wet cheek.

"Let's go to Allen's house."

"What?" Luke nearly shrieked.

"Just take me there. I purchased every item therein, and, by God, I'm going to make use of it."

Luke shrugged. "Someone has to, I guess."

"You guessed right."

It wasn't long until they'd reached the porch he'd whitewashed all those weeks ago.

She entered the house with Luke right behind her. Walking into the kitchen, Beatrice filled four huge soup pots with water and set them to boil on the stove.

"Er, Peaches, what are you doing?"

She smiled and crooked a finger at him. She led him to a room that held a porcelain, claw-footed bathtub. "You see, I need someone to scrub my back," she purred and leaned into him.

"And someone to carry the water?" he asked sardonically.

"How sweet of you to volunteer," she teased.

* * * *

The next morning Beatrice stood in the lobby of the Grand Hotel with a carpet bag in each hand, waiting for Luke to come down with his father and brother. Her eyelids drooped as she remembered the night before. They'd bathed by candlelight and, after he had carried her across the yard and back to her own bed, they'd made love all night long.

A lazy grin spread across her face as she recalled all the luscious things they'd done to each other, the things he'd taught her, the positions he'd had her in. Shivering, she took a deep breath and exhaled dreamily. It had been the first time they'd slept in each other's arms in the privacy of a home, as God intended.

The Hughson men descended the stairs and greeted her, each in his own flirtatious style. She counted herself lucky she was to be a part of Luke's handsome family.

There were three stages to take the party to the train depot in Tucson, and, after a wonderful farewell from their friends the Clarks, the Whites and the McElroys, they were off. Luke and Beatrice had their own carriage, Mr Hughson, Mr Wendell, and Governor

Frémont shared the second one, and, she imagined, Rory had the third all to himself.

"I suppose your father thinks me a hoyden for my behaviour," Beatrice commented as they topped the first hill on the way to Tucson.

Luke shrugged. "Until I reminded him that he and my mother had relations before they were married."

Beatrice felt a shock go through her. "And how do you know this?"

"Years ago, just before I left for school, my dear father dropped me off at my first—er—*boarding house*."

"Really? Do go on."

"More or less, he confessed such in a conversation we'd had about women along the way."

"Where is your mother now?"

"Mother passed on during my first year at Columbia," he stated quietly.

She noted the flicker of remorse that passed over his features, but it disappeared as quickly as it had come. Her future husband was a pillar of strength, he always had been. She placed her hand on his arm. "I'm so sorry. She was a lovely woman, from what I recall."

Luke nodded, then turned to her. "You'll be the first lady in the house since she died, lucky for us. Those boys back there are in need of some manners."

Smiling softly, she lifted her hand and touched his cheek. "Your father and brother do just fine, don't you worry about them."

"Fine? They are terrible flirts—and with *my* woman!"

She chuckled. "As if I could love anyone else but you."

Luke pulled her into his arms. "I've finally drawn the Queen of Hearts, Peaches." Then he kissed her.

About the Author

Born and reared in Southern California, Genella deGrey longed to be your typical blonde, tanned, surfer girl but failed miserably. Unable to sit idle without falling asleep, she embarked upon several artistic endeavours. Make-up and set dressing for the entertainment industry, Resort Enhancement for The Walt Disney Company and writing sexy historical romance top the list of her favourite activities. A consummate closet goth and amateur music and (red) wine enthusiast, she is also a hopeless romantic awaiting the arrival of her very own Mr Romance/Soul Mate with whom to share the rest of her life.

Come and visit her on the web at genelladegrey.com

Genella DeGrey loves to hear from readers. You can find her contact information, website details and author profile page at http://www.total-e-bound.com.

Total-E-Bound Publishing

www.total-e-bound.com

Take a look at our exciting range of literagasmic™
erotic romance titles and discover pure quality
at Total-E-Bound.